A Kind of Drownin

A Kind of Drowning

by

Robert Craven

A Kind of Drowning

Copyright ©Robert Craven 2021

All rights reserved. No part of this book may be reproduced, stored in a retrieval system or transmitted in any form by any means without prior written permission of the publisher or author, except by a reviewer who may quote brief passages in a review to be printed in a newspaper, magazine or journal.

The right of Robert Craven to be identified as the author of this work has been asserted by him/her in accordance with the Copyright Designs and Patents Act 1988.

The novel is a work of fiction. The names and characters are the product of the author's imagination and resemblance to actual persons, living or dead, is entirely coincidental. Objections to the content of this book should be directed towards the author and owner of the intellectual property rights as registered with their local government.

Cover Design

Cover design by Design for Writers ©2021

A Kind of Drowning

For Dr. Jacky Collins

A Kind of Drowning

By
Robert Craven:

The wartime adventures of Eva Molenaar:

Get Lenin

Zinnman

A finger of night

Hollow Point

Eagles Hunt Wolves
(winner of the Firebird Award 2021)

Steampunk:

The Mandarin Cipher: A Wentworth & Devereux adventure

Holt:

The Road of a Thousand Tigers

A Kind of Drowning

My heartfelt thanks to:

Sue Procter at thinkforensic.co.uk
for her time and suggestions.

Thalassophobia – The persistent and intense fear of bodies of deep, dark water and of what exists below the surface…

> *"What a fearful thing it is when the voyager sets forth, but a curse remains behind."*
>
> **Wole Soyinka**

Midnight

They were waiting for him outside his penthouse,. Two hoodlums built like brick shithouses draped in the street and topped off by identical black NYC peaked caps. One blocks him at the entrance to the foyer, saying he recognised him from the news. The one from behind blindsides him with a rabbit punch, knocking his sunglasses across the deserted pavement. Buckled to his knees then frog-marched across the car park to the waiting car, he is unceremoniously tossed onto the back seat. His i-Phone is confiscated. On the journey, with his head tilted back, nose pinched, trying to staunch the flow of blood down his tailored shirt, he can hear them debating their next music project: A 'Mad Dub Irish K-Pop vibe'. The heavy sets of rings and chains glint as they waved their hands about. The only way he can tell them apart is one has tattoos on the knuckles (now laced with his blood) and one has not. They spark up their spliffs with an 18 carat gold Boucheron lighter. Funny the details you remember.

"T.T., TakeTwo?" *says the one who had rabbit-punched him.*

A Kind of Drowning

"*That's shite,*" *replies the other one,* "*What about T.M.? Twin mix?*"

"*Sounds like a Twix, bro,*" *grins Mr. Blindside.*

Sounds like a whole lot of wank, he thinks. He envies the driver, screened off from the haze and the incoherent chatter. The taste of blood mixes with the heavy noxious smoke at the back of his throat and he thinks he is going to vomit. On and on through the drive Tweedle Dum and Tweedle Dee yammer until they settle on something incomprehensible as the title for their album.

They fist bump across him with solemn nods.

He finds himself on board the boat. Well, 'Boat' doesn't even begin to do it justice. Boat suggests something small with oars or possibly a sail. This was a sleek white luxury motor yacht, cutting out to sea like a machete running on serious horsepower.

The two thugs strong-arm him down onto the middle chair, pinioning his arms to a table as they sit either side. He finds himself facing the unblinking expression of the luxury vessel's owner.

"*Try not to get any blood on anything, yeah?*" *says the big man.* His life vest over his weatherproof jacket makes him look like a spinning top. They are sitting aft on the deck.

"*That suit of yours needs to go back to the bloody tailors, mate,*" *he continues.*

His suit? wondering if something was out of place, untidy, a loose button?

"*What...*" *he blinks,*

"*The pockets.*"

"*...What about them?*"

"*Your fingers can't reach the bottom...*" *intones the burly man,* "*...can't reach the change.*"

A Kind of Drowning

He and his two assailants got the gag and laugh.

But the big guy isn't laughing.

"You've an outstanding invoice, the old T's and C's, T's, and C's, I'm afraid" he states matter-of-factly.

The tattooed hand one finds this even funnier. A row of teeth flashed, they looked almost too big for the mouth. The giggle sounds girlish. Girlish like a chainsaw.

With an old tissue tamped up each nostril it finally dawns on him: Invoice. Unpaid bills.

The big man facing him has a lilt, the way the vowels got stretched, Australian at times, Dublin inner city next. Beyond the lights of the overhead canopy, blackness lies beyond. Blackness and the unforgiving depths of The Irish Sea where his iPhone now resides.

"My people will look after that,"

"No. You. Will." The big man sighs.

"I don't have the cash to hand – how did you find me anyway?"

"You're all over social media, you moron, partying all over the town. Now we're into 5k a week penalties, which brings you to one hundred and forty five grand, let's round it up to one hundred and fifty thousand, due now, today, sport,"

The big man mashes his hands together as if in prayer. Two meaty index fingers spired.

He finds his voice now, "You can fuck off,"

"I'm not the one sitting here with a face like a butcher's block," says the big man whose patience is rapidly wearing thin,

"Don't have it. Simple as."

"Find it,"

"*What part of 'Fuck off' do you not understand?*" he croaks. *Air seems to evaporate out of his lungs.*

"*You have a safety deposit box in Adelaide Road. Private and exclusive.*"

He has two safety deposit boxes at two separate locations in Dublin city, supposed to be confidential. He stares in disbelief at the unblinking mass of flesh.

"*Yes, I have,*" he says.

"*In that safety deposit box, you have a collection of Rolexes. I'll take two. Early birthday presents for my two beauts here. Nothing like that crappy timepiece on your wrist.*"

For his size, the big guy was whip-snap fast. He lurches across the table, spilling empty beer bottles and pint glasses. A left arm is wrenched up and the cuff pulled down.

"*Nice – Omega?*"

"*It's a Seamaster,*"

"*It's a piece of shit. A bit like you, a shiny bit of fucking useless tat,*"

A severe headache was slowly spreading across his skull from the from the beating, the motion of the boat and the tendons popping like fireworks in his compressed wrist. His bowels are beginning to churn. The cold is biting into him. He dry-heaves but only some spittle clings to his lips. He spits it onto the deck, carefully avoiding the expensive looking rug beneath the chairs.

His three tormentors stare in disgust. He tries to bundle himself deeper into the expensive Italian fabric.

The big man, unwrapping his grip, holds his two palms face up.

"*You're a little gurrier like me; simple as. We're playing by Dublin rules, as in, there are none, sport. No-holds-barred MMA. Small print, those pesky T's and C's apply,*"

A Kind of Drowning

The boat slows gradually, bumping along the swells towards an aged stone jetty. Waves buffet the yacht. One of the beauts, the tattooed one, leaps onto the jetty and bounds toward the moorings.

"Now, you're going to give me a guided tour. It has potential I can see that. Your solicitor is one of my clients and being a moron like you, had forgotten about the t's and c's," the big man continues, "He gave this gig up after my boys here paid a visit. We were going to bring him along tonight on this little jaunt. Make it cosy like, only he's recently developed breathing difficulties and is indisposed. I want a share of this. Silent partner, sport, yeah?"

Then he find his guts. He spews them heartily over the deck before clambering to puke over the gunwale.

"And if you try to fuck me over. We'll pay that pretty little gal of yours a visit. Film it, upload it to Porn Hub. Dark Net shit. Be a gas," says the big man.

The trio hoist him up onto the concrete and then march him up the ancient worn stone. His legs give out and he collapses onto the jetty. Staring up, he thinks the lights of Dublin blink as far away as the distant constellations above,

"Yes, this will do nicely," says the big man, "very nicely indeed," as they make their way up the jetty.

The rest of the night is a blur to him, only revealed through nightmarish flashes.

He knows the boat is moored in the Poolbeg Marina, on the river Liffey, near the bustling docks of Dublin. Secure in its private berth it's getting cleaned down. Removing his smatterings of blood and vomit stains.

A Kind of Drowning

1

"Where to, Boss?"

It was Crowe's kind of ride, neither he nor the taxi driver spoke. The sporadic bursts from the Satnav punctuated the silence. Dublin's suburbs gave way to the northbound motorway.

But long distances abhor a vacuum,

"I know you," she said.

Crowe flicked his eyes across the laminated ID – the driver's name was Abosede Akande O'Hare. He spied the small camera on the mirror behind a thick-beaded wooden rosary hanging from the mirror.

"I don't think I've had the pleasure," he replied.

"You look done in," she said.

He drew his hand across the week long stubble then pulled it away; he studied it. The knuckles still had faint traces of bruising. He covered them with his other hand. Sometimes the tremors arrived unannounced. The scratches had healed in coarse diagonal lines. A faint indentation on his finger hinted where a wedding band used to be.

Crowe had gone twenty-four hours without sleep. He had the kind of sour hangover that felt like a vice squeezing in on either side of his skull.

The white lines of the road were hypnotic. A passing truck flicked its lights like a flashgun sending lightening forks across his prefrontal cortex.

A lot could change in a fortnight, he thought.

"You police?" asked Abosede.

"No," Crowe replied.

Abosede made a clicking sound with her tongue, rolling the words "PJ, PJ, PJ.." like a rolodex.

She turned her flawless profile scanning him up and down. She saw a man in an unwashed fleece; a man whose entire existence was stuffed into pockets and bags.

"You look like police," she murmured.

"It's *Gardai* in this country,"

"Gard*ee*. Guarding what?" she snorted.

Guarding what indeed, he thought.

"I'm paying you only to drive," said Crowe.

The clicking continued, she mumbled something under her breath. It sounded like *"Stronger air freshener,"*

He couldn't be sure.

The cab smelled exotic. A gold watch glowed on her ebony skin; its glass was covered in a faint meshwork of cracks.

"Not paying me enough," she said.

Crowe slunk further into his seat.

Twelve junctions later, the northbound motorway siphoned off to a dual carriageway that dog-legged onto a secondary road. The silence stretched out to forever. The first signposts for his destination appeared.

"Well, don't expect any sunshine in Roscarrig, man. The forecast for the summer is terrible," said Abosede.

"Suits me, I've been told to rest," said Crowe.

"You cannot rest in Dublin?"

"No-one seems to think so," he paused, pressing his forehead against the window. The faint vibrations of the road coursed through his temples, "I thought I'd get away,"

"Why? The city is where the money is, the money is boss; it crisp, it nice,"

He closed his eyes,

"I could tell you, but then I'd have to kill you," he said.

"I *do* know you. Brutality, man. Brutality," said Abosede.

Like her photo, her braids were piled gloriously high on her head.

"Roscarrig, thanks. No more talk or I will definitely kill you," he replied.

Crowe's gaze fell onto the glove compartment, an adhesive 3-D Jesus doled out a plastic benediction. Abosede glanced sideways at him,

"*Believe in the Lord Jesus and you will be saved*," she intoned,

"I never trust anyone who's read just one book," said Crowe.

The silence descended between them like a pall.

Dilapidated lines of greenhouses amid large tracts of grass, yellow gorse and seas of ragwort sailed past,

"*Jacobaea Vulgaris,*" he muttered.

He thought about Googling the word *ragwort*, but like his watch, the blood stained mobile phone was sealed tight and locked away in an evidence bag.

He folded his arms.

Abosede's tongue started clicking again.

A Kind of Drowning

Two bedraggled roundabouts later, they passed a peeling, dirty reflective welcome sign that requested everyone to please drive slowly. The Satnav announced that they had reached their destination. They were on the narrow main street of Roscarrig town.

It was a town dismal and forgotten; out of time and out of luck, thought Crowe. The ragged end of nowhere.

Last stop, he thought.

His destination, Gallagher Estates, had a collage of lettings and sales in its polished shopfront window. The façade was pock-marked with flaking paintwork, darkened by years of HGV diesel fumes. The paving at the front dipped giving the building an air of sagging slowly into the ground.

Crowe peeled off a few twenties for Abosede from a crumpled looking leather tan wallet. He had €200 in it, and €3000 in a money belt, the last of his savings. She smiled a gap-toothed thanks; a semi-precious stone glittered in one of her incisors. Looking around, she scowled,

"This miserable place is nowhere, man. Got no chance of a fare back 'til the city," she said.

He added another fifty Euro to her fare,

"I only plan to stay here for a week, maybe two," replied Crowe.

"In a malevolent *no*-place like this? A lifetime, man," she replied.

From an animal print purse, she handed him a business card. It was pristine white and bisected by a thin grey cross,

"My brother has a meeting place, a mission. You welcome anytime,"

"Is that your mobile number along the bottom?" asked Crowe.

"Yes," she replied.

Soup and salvation. He jammed the card into the pocket of his fleece. The last thing he needed was a lifeline.

Crowe hauled himself out of the taxi and removed his big sports holdall and a backpack. Abosede looked up and down the main street and executed a brisk three-point-turn.

"You do not tarry, man. Do not delay," she shouted out the window to Crowe.

In the past thirty-six hours, Crowe had abandoned the vape and started mainlining nicotine via the pack of B&H King size 20's. A spring breeze idled up the main street, tinged with salt and cutting to the bone forcing him to cup his hands around the lighter. Crowe shut his eyes, took a deep pull, revelling in the momentary darkness and then he heard the shop door open. Opening his eyes he saw a tall man come out to meet him. Crowe could see that the man's well-pressed suit was a decade out of date.

"Gallagher?" asked Crowe.

"That's me. Are you alright?" he asked.

Crowe shifted the weight of his holdall.

"You look like you've come to relax," continued Gallagher.

"I've come here to recover," replied Crowe.

"I can see that. Quigley was worried about you. I've given my secretary, Hilary, an extended lunch. We can talk in the privacy of my office. Is it Pius, John or PJ?"

Crowe thought about Abosede's mantra,

"John."

"John it is then," said Gallagher, "I'm Derry."

His handshake looked as slippery as his smile.

Crowe ignored the proffered hand. He dropped the half-finished smoke onto the cracked pavement and crushed it.

"Come inside," said Gallagher.

The office was small, painted in faded tangerine. The atmosphere was a combination of damp, strong perfume, and Chinese food smells. The desk beside Gallagher's, presumably Hilary's, was a shining testament to optimism; perched on top of the monitor was a soft toy – a reindeer with a red 'Merry Christmas' jumper.

"How do you want to play this – off the books, John?" he asked. Despite the nonchalance, Gallagher seemed nervous and alert.

"Preferably. The less paper the better – cash?" said Crowe.

"Of course. Now, John, I'll be brutally honest, it's not much, a garret basically with all the mod cons. Though, it will become a premium Airbnb let after June. Double the rental in fact." Gallagher tapped his laptop keyboard as if he were headlining Carnegie Hall. No rings, but a solid block of metal watch peeped out of his starched cuffs with novelty blue enamel cuff links of crossed golf clubs.

"Help yourself," he said, following Crowe's gaze.

A black and chrome coffee machine shone in pride of place beside a stack of disposable cups. Crowe crushed rather than inserted the pod. Viscous black coffee oozed into the cup.

"How is that old reprobate Quigley, still singing?" asked Gallagher.

"I think so, yes," said Crowe.

A Kind of Drowning

Small UHT milk pots and sugar sachets stood to attention beside a shiny teaspoon. Crowe tore and crushed to get the hit he needed. He used all the milk pots and piled them into the bin.

There was a basic office chair facing the desk. Derry Gallagher liked to conduct brisk business. The metal and plastic sighed under Crowe's weight.

The small cream-coloured printer at Gallagher's elbow began whirring into life.

"Let's start with a month's rent. Cash. Right now?" said Crowe.

"That would certainly do it." Gallagher grinned.

Crowe stood and opened a money belt. It seemed to offer underwire support to his gut. He handed it to Gallagher.

"Could you hold on to this, I'd like to make withdrawals without drawing too much attention?"

"Business hours are 9am to 5:30," replied Gallagher. He pinched the belt between thumb and forefinger regarding it as if it were roadkill and placed it in the safe., "After 6pm, there's an after-hours surcharge,"

"I'll bear that in mind," replied Crowe.

With a flourish, Gallagher handed over the print-out.

"I see Quigley is the owner / occupier on the lease?" said Crowe.

"He bought it ten years ago."

"Trust Quigley to find somewhere completely anonymous and off-the-grid in twenty-first century Ireland," murmured Crowe.

He shifted his weight in the chair as he drained the last of his coffee. The frame gave a warning crack and a groan. Gallagher glanced over in concern,

"Tell you what, John, I'll take you out for lunch, show you around and then take you to your new digs. My shout. Throw the luggage in the boot."

He give the chair a good lash of the disinfectant wipe as Crowe reached for his bags.

Roscarrig was as Crowe expected, a mix of aged thatch cottages and tightly packed 1950's two storey pebble dash houses fighting for any available space along the main street. TO LET signs hung over a line of shuttered premises where Gallagher's Lexus was parked in a disabled spot. A church, local community centre, two pubs, Chinese takeaways, Polski Sklep, Post Office and a bookies flowed past the passenger window. A corner shop festooned with floral hanging baskets made a heroic attempt at a little local colour. Its wares were arranged in wooden trays on metal trestles beneath white cursive that stated – *'Today's specials'*.

"Eleven years ago, Roscarrig had a population of fifteen hundred. Today, its ten thousand – mostly starter homes. Commuter-belt first-time buyers. It's a ghost town between seven am and five-thirty. I can recommend the golf course," said Gallagher.

"Don't play it," replied Crowe.

"A man should have a hobby – we have a library, a good one, I believe. We have a local GAA club, a rowing club on the outskirts, but that's about it. Food-wise it's the usual haute cuisine of burgers and chips or cattery-chow-mein if that's your thing, though a new café has opened facing the Harbour – The Boogie-Woogie, great open prawn sandwiches."

A Kind of Drowning

The main street wove past a stone horseshoe harbour where a few small fishing boats, skiffs and larger trawlers sat moored. A latticework of ropes held them tightly to the harbour wall. The road meandered along lines of fields where labourers toiled in bright Day-Glo, amid muddied John Deeres and canvas sided trailers. It snaked along the coast for several miles. Long lines of houses, new builds and estates were pocketed suddenly amid the fields, giving the whole town a loosely assembled appearance. A train station and an Aldi supermarket marked the town's outer boundary. A simple graveyard with a ruined old church stood sentinel on the border and the road disappeared over a rise to the next town of Farandore.

Crowe glanced at his watch only to remember he didn't have one.

Not anymore.

"It's always been a small fishing town, really. If you're up early enough you can purchase some of the catch when the boats come in. And over this rise, the piece de resistance; Inishcarrig," said Gallagher.

They pulled up to a dusty, worn-out siding bordered by nettles.

It was a large island, several miles across. A Martello tower and compact old house were visible on the western lee. Behind it, shrouded in mist close to the horizon was the two-tone markings of a light house. Fishing boats bisected the channel between Inishcarrig and the mainland, laying out nets and lobster pots. Orange markers bobbed in the currents. The sun fought its way through the gloom, dappling the island in yellows, greens, and rich ambers. Crowe filled his lungs with sea air.

The possibility of summer rolled around his chest.

Gallagher viewed the island like an unrequited love,

"It's owned by the Canadian property billionaire, Richard Norcott. Messy divorce, wife wants half of his fortune, new high-maintenance squeeze and rumour has it, Inishcarrig is on the negotiating table. Now, I'm starving – let's hit the Boogie-Woogie Café," said Gallagher.

He launched the Lexus into a sharp reverse. Grinding the gears, Gallagher slid the car onto the road and accelerated toward the town. The stone harbour came into view.

2

Situated on a street corner, the Boogie-Woogie Café offered two views from the high plate glass windows: the harbour with the moored trawlers and the stretch of sea to Inishcarrig. The walls had an eclectic array of kitsch gelato posters and fading French lavender fields mounted on the faux-brick walls. Tables and chairs were closely packed across the dark parquet floor. The crowd was mostly elderly, female, and huddled in chattering groups. One had a yappy Pomeranian. It seemed to want to join in the conversations. A plexi-glass counter displayed an array of pastries, savouries, and sandwiches. A slate menu board offered today's specials scrawled in multi-coloured chalk. If Roscarrig was slowly checking out on the gurney, The Boogie-Woogie Café was the last bright pulse on the monitor.

"Sorry for the delay, lads, the kitchen porter didn't bother showing up today," said the waitress. She had an oriental-themed tattoo sleeve on one arm, the three surgical plasters on the other suggested she was going for a full house. A spider had been etched below her heavily pierced right ear. A severe ponytail stretched her features and her eyes were set to default bored.

Crowe momentarily thought the spider had come to life. He fought the sudden unease.

"Lauren, isn't it?" asked Gallagher.

"Uh huh," replied Lauren.

"I was here yesterday, Derry. Derry Gallagher,"

"Yeah… I remember – you had the special. Any craic?" said Lauren.

"No – you?" grinned Gallagher.

Lauren looked around,

"We've a new girl starting this week. You'll love her, the Farrell girl. Thea. Total sweetheart."

The chatter of life and the feel-good ambience made Crowe feel stronger than he had in five weeks, when the days had felt like slipping into deep dark water, without any ray of light. He needed to get well again, get sharp and deal with the demons. He ordered a toasted three cheese on white with a side of fries. Coffee - black. He scoured the condiments and pulled two vinegar pouches, he commandeered the salt and nudged the offending pepper towards Gallagher.

Lauren jotted the order down. Pulled a beeping mobile out of her tight jeans. Made a very teenage moue. Scrolled. Stabbed the screen with her thumb and then wandered over to the next table.

Gallagher took the napkin and wiped the cutlery down. Once that task was completed, he wiped the place mat and the area around it.

"I'm fine, thanks," said Crowe.

Gallagher sighed, a little miffed.

A sudden commotion outside made everyone look up. One of the tables on the terrace was attacked by a trio of seagulls. They circled, swooped, and landed on the table stamping and scattering plates, coffee mugs and cutlery. The startled couple leapt out of their seats to the feral shrieks of the birds. A contest of flapping, feinting, swiping, dodging, and squawking ensued. The woman, swinging her handbag connected with one of the gulls, clattering it into the window. The glass shuddered from the impact.

The conversations around the café slowly piped up, but the Pomeranian remained silent.

"Never seen that before," said Gallagher.

"Never a dull moment," said Crowe,

The food arrived. Crowe drenched the fries in vinegar. He emptied three sachets of sugar into the Americano.

"Three's my lucky number, Derry," he said.

Gallagher stared back in horror,

"Type-2 diabetes doesn't worry you then?" he said.

"Nope," mumbled Crowe forcing the sandwich into his mouth. A smear of cheese was pushed aside by the heel of his hand.

They ate lost in their own thoughts amid the shrill and raucous laughter of contented retirement, punctuated by subdued Pomeranian yaks.

Gallagher paid the bill, swiping his card like a magic wand. He didn't give a tip and requested a receipt which he carefully folded into a square. With a cheery wave to the septuagenarian audience, they drove to Crowe's new digs.

Which lived up to Gallagher's billing. Perched on top of a Chinese takeaway named The Dragon Inn, it was small. A bedsit with loftier ambitions. The ceiling was white with inset lights, the walls were a matt magnolia and the flooring looked bargain laminate. That said, the garret-cum-bedsit looked clean and well maintained and smelled of mild citrus detergent. Microwave, gas hob, tiny electric oven, pocket-sized fridge, and a leather settee, it reminded Crowe of a VW camper on breeze blocks.

"Fold-out sofa bed, electric shower is in the bathroom," said Gallagher.

A sofa-bed. Crowe's spine began to protest at the prospect.

A small flat screen TV was mounted on the wall over an old empty fireplace. Two radiators ensured that if necessary, the winter would be snug. A skylight fitted into the ceiling brought the onshore breezes in.

The other window, overlooking a neglected courtyard promised fried rice and grease smells daily.

"Day or night, I'm on the end of a phone, John; any friend of Quigs is a friend of mine," he said.

Gallagher must have really, really fucked up somewhere along the line to have Quigley as a friend.

"If you need anything else?" asked Gallagher.

"No. Thank you," replied Crowe.

Gallagher offered a sweaty hand and this time Crowe shook it.

"See you 'round, Squire," said Gallagher.

Crowe folded out his hold-all and began his new life stacking shelves with T-shirts, underwear, and socks. He ran a cold, cold shower to wake himself from the stupor of existence. He glanced in the mirror and looked away; he'd hunt down a disposable razor in the supermarket some other time. Reaching into his pocket, Crowe found the twist of coke, the wrapping smeared with his fingerprints. He'd been given the gram as he had left the HR hearing. Union Rep Harris had his uses. He wiped the packet clean and searching around, hid it under the S-bend of the toilet – easy to flush should the need ever arise.

Crowe lit up his cigarette from the gas hob. Looking around for the source of the rapidly increasing beeps of the smoke alarm, he found it over the hob, pulled it apart and prised out the battery. Then he filled the electric kettle and rummaged around the shelves for a teabag.

He thought about the kitchen porter who hadn't shown up for work at the Boogie-Woogie. The less he saw of Gallagher, the happier his recuperation would be.

3

Sleep had eluded Crowe. Past cases had forced their way into his head, denying him rest. Fighting the rising sensation of being overwhelmed, he folded up the sofa bed and put the kettle on. From the cupboard, he took out a jar of instant coffee. He looked up at the clock on the wall. 3am, the midnight of the soul, the time when death usually came knocking. The clock with *"Time for tea"* in cheery cursive tried its best to bring some colour to the beige banality. The smoke alarm battery offered an object to rotate on the kitchen table in tight circles. When he got bored with that, he paced out the room; fourteen paces long by six paces wide. After several mulling circuits, Crowe sat and smoked, he drank the cold milky coffee, and spun a cheap red plastic lighter. The remains of last night's meal, a large single of chips from the take-away, lay folded on the table. Its greasy smell lingered in the pokey kitchen. Some of it remained cloying in his beard.

Crowe shut his eyes, but no matter how hard he tried, the past unfurled like a ghost appearing at the banquet. He pictured the Internal Affairs members around the kitchen table like an instant replay, he inched his hand protectively toward the crumpled chip bag.

Hungry bastards.

"What were you thinking, Garda Inspector Crowe?" asked Crowe's superior, Chief Superintendent Dáithí O'Suilleabháin; – the ramrod-straight Cork man who strode through the office everyday like he was lining out for an All-Ireland final.

Beside O'Suilleabháin, the head of HR, Stephanie Townsend had sat angular and ironed into her sombre suit.

"Hardly Champions League now was it, Inspector Crowe?" said Townsend.

The tapes had been rolling. Her withering gaze didn't flinch as Crowe had said his piece at the top of his lungs.

Sitting beside him was his Union Rep, Harris, who was making a careful study of his long thin spired fingers as the hearing became a spectacular one-man train wreck. He sat silent.

Crowe had got the gist from Townsend's cool reply – *Government front bench reshuffle last week, new Minister of Justice; Noirín Gartland; keen to make her mark; Sees herself as a new broom dealing with old male archetypes in the force. If Inspector Crowe had behaved appropriately and not lost his temper, his name and face wouldn't be appearing from here to Timbuktu.*

Crowe knew it. Harris knew it and O'Suilleabháin knew it too. THE BIG MACHINE had spoken, and in the space of a week after that informal investigation, the resolution was swift and brutal. He was out, suspended without pay for three months. He had needed cash; he had needed a phone.

He had needed to talk to Quigley.

Crowe shut his eyes, forcing himself into the now. His vision was watery when he opened them again.

"Well, that went well," he said out loud.

He looked up at the clock. The hours felt leaden and dawn fell heavy around his shoulders as it crept in through the window shades. He tried not to see the spiders scurrying in his peripheral vision or hear the whispering click-click weaving from their spinnerets in his shuttered mind.

All of a sudden, he wasn't sure where he was. He needed something tangible, some anchor to the day. Crowe felt a tug of envy at the sound of Roscarrig waking up; the chirrup of car alarms and over-revved engines departing for the rush hour, funnelled along the main street, pumped out like metallic beads onto the motorway. He didn't have a car of his own, not anymore. Trying to escape, he had glanced his VW off a stationary bus and collided with a tree. The marks of the airbag on his face had subsided somewhat, but shaving was still an exercise in torture.

His boxers hung limply around his hips, he had to hitch them up as he rose to rinse the plate and cup. Crowe swilled the remaining dregs and downed them in a gulp. Then he heard the bang of the outer door. A second later a cold blast of air wound its way through the garret and pinched at his toes.

He heard the lock turn.

Quigley let himself in,

"The place stinks. Would you open a window for Jaysus sake?" he said.

"…and how are you this fine morning, Quigley?" said Crowe.

Quigley's grey eyes took in the kitchen with a glance. His slicked back hair, now white, made him look like Marlon Brando. If you did well, it was 'son'. If you fucked-up, you were a 'pup'. Retired Garda Sergeant Proinsias Quigley's world was black and white.

"Living the dream, son," he said, "If you have a brew on…?"

Crowe searched for a second cup. He found a chipped one at the back of the shelf and blew off the dust. He rinsed it under the tap and pushed the extractor fan on. It wheezed into life.

From a plastic shopping bag, Quigley pulled out a mobile phone. It was an android with a charger, its lead was bound in a thick elastic band.

"Thanks for the help. The cash, this place." asked Crowe.

"I figured you'd need one of these too. This is the Wifi code for the apartment."

"Derry Gallagher tells me the reception is bad out here," said Crowe.

Quigley tossed the phone onto the table, his big hands sweeping the crumbs off, grabbing the chip bag, he put it in the pedal bin. He then spotted the battery lying on the table. Eyeing the mountain of butts in the saucer beside it, he sought out the smoke alarm. He unscrewed the alarm from its ceiling mounting and slammed home the battery. Pressing on the check button he smiled at the little squeak it emitted.

"Gallagher couldn't find his arse if his hands were tied behind his back. If you disconnect the smoke alarm again, P.J., you're out on the street, no messing, yeah?" said Quigley.

He slid the other kitchen chair over to the table. Leaning his elbows onto the surface, the table listed towards him.

"Any friends you can reach out to?" he asked.

One of the last of the old beat cops, Quigley had known all the safe houses, known all the characters. Nothing escaped him. He held his gaze until Crowe blinked. From the fleece hanging from the door, Crowe produced a letter. It was in a brown envelope with the official stamp of the harp.

He handed it to Quigley,

"Apart from you?" said Crowe.

Quigley opened out the letter.

Private and Confidential:

"In Accordance with S.I. 214 of 2007, Section 123 of The Garda Síochána Act 2005..."

"...*It is the opinion of the Garda Commissioner that on review of the disciplinary hearing...*"

Quigley skimmed to the punchline:

"*It is the decision of the Commissioner that you, Garda Inspector Pius John Crowe are hereby suspended for three months without pay for that duration, thereafter, to be reviewed on a date decided by the Commissioner...*"

"Murder Squad will be under pressure without you," said Quigley.

He handed it back to former Garda Inspector Pius John Crowe. It was a badge like a leper's bell.

"Not enough to stop them throwing me under the bus," replied Crowe.

"Grist to the mill for Mr-Páirc-Ui-Fucking-Chaoimh, O'Suilleabháin," said Quigley, "He probably has one of his goon squad already lined up to replace you,"

"They can answer all the reporters' questions in my inbox then. I appreciate the phone, Quigley" said Crowe, "mine was confiscated."

"Internal Affairs are just being thorough, son. Have you seen a doctor yet?" asked Quigley.

"Yep. I was handed over to the tender mercies of the GOHS; full medical, bloods, the lot," said Crowe

"Care to elaborate?" replied Quigley.

Cholesterol was off the chart, but whose wasn't these days?

"No. I'm suffering from severe stress. Review after next hearing," said Crowe.

"I read the papers, watched the news, heard the Garda Union chatter. What exactly did you do?" he asked.

"This went up a few days ago, you'll love it," said Crowe, "updated and pure Scorsese. Hand me your phone."

A Google search brought the YouTube link up straight away. He handed it back to Quigley.

Quigley stared at the footage: Crowe landing the first punch, a haymaker followed by a succession of fast, hard jabs on the U-14s soccer coach. The same scene at various angles was jump-cut and spliced into a sequence showing not only Crowe bearing down on the smaller unconscious man in an ecstasy of rage, but also the expressions on the faces of the children on both teams.

Including Crowe's son, Cathal. He stood; shoulders slumped. He had spent weeks perfecting his goal celebration, insisting that Crowe watch. Instead Cathal watched his father hammer into the man who had waved and complained that Cathal's goal was off-side.

"You used your phone on the poor bastard," said Quigley, "That was overkill."

"Don't remember any of it," said Crowe,

"I don't think yer man there will remember much after that battering," said Quigley, "That has rehab stamped all over it."

He handed back the phone.

"Meds?" he asked.

Crowe glanced at the closed toilet door. Quigley noticed it too.

"I don't need them," Crowe replied.

"You'll have to play the game, son. Counselling, Occupational Health, the whole fucking shebang – who's your Union Rep?"

"Harris. Phoenix Park."

"That fucking pup?". He shook his head. "You're not the main reason I'm in town to be honest - do you know Desmond Cosgrave?"

He let the sentence hang.

"*The* Desmond Cosgrave? Teflon D?" replied Crowe. He tried to recall the criminal record, the details, "missing a thumb?"

"The same, lost it to a China man over an unpaid heroin bill," said Quigley.

"Didn't the Chinese dealer go missing?" replied Crowe. Somewhere at the back of his mind, in the shattered recesses, a touch paper fuse had been lit. An ember in a cavern.

Teflon D, a name created by the tabloids, a netherworld criminal moniker that was both flattering and damning. All of Teflon's ilk were the same; five rings of fat neck supporting a bullet-shaped skull. All T-shirt, tattoos, Kevlar bullet-proof vest and black ADIDAS pants. Production line villainy.

"The guy's a toe rag, what's he doing out here?" continued Crowe.

"Pissed off some of the city gangs, I'm a messenger from The Park. Personal, like. He survived a gang attack three weeks ago; the family home was burned out. Two BMWs torched belonging to the sons, Setanta and Fionn; those faded glory boyband idiots turned narcotics dispensers. Poor old Teflon's Merc, a high-performance government model shipped in from Latvia went up like a Roman candle. The story was in the papers?"

"I avoid the papers," replied Crowe.

A Kind of Drowning

"The old guard are being taken out. You've seen it yourself; the new gangs are a different breed. Kevlar isn't going to be much use to him. Explains why he's out here."

Quigley continued, "Wouldn't want to be gasping for a cuppa?"

Crowe steadied himself against his chair and launched toward the sink. Everything felt like slow motion; he felt he was wading through treacle. As he began to fill the kettle, his right hand began to shake uncontrollably, and he dropped it. It bounced across the floor, spewing water. He stared at it blankly.

Quigley walked over and filled it. He handed it to Crowe who stared at the kettle as if for the first time. He sensed at that moment, most if not all of his functions were wired incorrectly. He felt useless. Then he remembered it needed plugging in.

Quigley was about to pass a remark, when he stared off into space for a minute, then let out a barrage of sudden loud sneezes. In reflex, he muffled them in the crook of his elbow,

"Fuckin' flu coming on," he said,

He ran the hot water tap, washing his hands vigorously. He dried his hands with a sheet of paper towel. He shook himself and was about to place a hand on Crowe's shoulder, then stopped. He slotted his thumbs into the belt loops of his jeans instead; Superman's dad laid low,

"It's just a speed-bump, son. A pin prick in your life. None of this will matter in six months. Get some exercise, seriously, you look like shit. Breathe for fuck's sake. Thanks for the tea by the way,"

"I haven't made it yet."

"Exactly, son."

The door closed as silently as it had opened. The outer door clanged shut and the *bruup* of a car alarm drifted in through the windows.

A Kind of Drowning

Crowe wondered how many more rubs he'd get off the lamp before Quigley would cut him loose to fend for himself. Sometimes small favours came at a heavy price. A friendship driven by misdirected brotherhood and loyalty.

The kettle came to a boil and Crowe shook himself as it switched off with a languid click.

4

YOU ARE A VALUABLE HUMAN BEING!

The web page pulsed an option, Crowe's thumb hovered over the new smartphone's screen. Beneath the banner a generic stock-shot of a man in a suit sitting in an office chair holding his head in his hands. A more accurate depiction would be an unkempt, overweight middle-aged man clad in boxers and in need of a shave. Not some well-groomed slightly concerned looking all-American stockbroker.

'What triggered this crisis?' said the voice at the end of the line. Her name was Patricia.

He had held off for a week, but after Quigley's morning visit, Crowe decided to ring the support-line number on the bottom of the web page. Play the game. Show you're willing to rehabilitate. A receptionist in soft tones had immediately directed him to Patricia once he'd given his name. Seems notoriety had its plusses, thought Crowe. They were now at Question 10 of 25 to ascertain whether he needed one-to-one counselling. Up to this point, each question, asked in a neutral tone, had a response range of one-to-five, to assess where his mind was – one was good, five was bad. So far, he had been hitting all the fives.

Q.10. The Trigger. Take your pick, he thought:

Christmas last year, standing in the rain-sodden carpark of a GAA club looking at a gangland victim who used to have a head now just bloodied meat from the business end of a semi-automatic. The defunct and ruined Kevlar vest cost twice as much as Crowe made in a month. The cheap stroller lying on its side amid the gore, a creche run cut horrifically short.

Or the homeless woman found dead behind a wheelie bin in the city, throat slashed with both breasts cut-off and missing; that cheery detail omitted from the press due to *'on-going operational reasons'*; subtext: a possible serial killer finding his raison d'être and everyone holding their breath waiting for Act 2.

How about the clown in the suburbs, whacked out on spice, using a claw hammer on his pretty girlfriend's head for a few hours before turning himself in? Dublin Murder Metropolitan served up a fresh smorgasbord of chaos every day.

But Alison's affair, *that* probably kick-started the spiral. Her sixteen-hour shifts as a midwife that put her into the orbit of a consultant who looked remarkably like 'Mr. Concerned' on the webpage. Shared medical crises had led to a 'fling' in her words. A fling that continued for nearly a year, leading to hissed exchanges and muttered recriminations while Cathal was at football training. Crowe took it on the chin. They had continued treading water in rostered work shifts, orbiting each other in sullen Catholic silence.

Alison had shown him the door. Suspension from duty was the final straw. Sixteen years of marriage sinking in front of him like the Titanic.

And the lifeboats were all at sea.

Cathal, the one bright spot in the marriage, had blanked him on the stairs lined with family photographs and wouldn't make eye-contact. His headphones an audio cocoon to match his downward stare. Crowe had tried to talk to him, tried to get him to listen, to *understand*. Without thinking, Crowe had yanked the headphones off and stamped on them in fury. Sweat and spittle ran off his face and chin.

Cathal had stared back in wide eyed terror inching his way back up the stairs. Wide-eyed terror.

 Alison had shielded him, placing herself between them. Hands held out in defence she stood on her tiptoes to eye Crowe,

"I'm changing the locks," she had said in the cool, distant voice that Crowe knew as marital purgatory, "You can fuck off with yourself, now. You're a lunatic, Crowe. Don't pack. Just. Go!"

He thought about the ten unanswered texts to Alison and Cathal. Separation papers were probably migrating across Dublin, flocking with the circling lawsuits, seeking him slowly out.

"Question 10, not sure what triggered it, Patricia. Something stupid, truth be told. My son's football team had suffered a losing streak, their first goal in ten games was disallowed. I snapped," said Crowe.

Patricia remained silent. She let the pause drift. Crowe lit a B&H.

"Next question – Question 11 – just a yes-or-no. Do you smoke?" she asked. Must have ESP, he thought. He shook the BIC as it was beginning to gutter gas. He lobbed it toward the kitchen bin where the smoke alarm battery resided. It struck the metal like a gong.

"Recently quit," replied Crowe

"Question 12 – Do you drink?"

"Yes. But only on weekends," he said.

"How many units per week?" Patricia's voice drifted; she was clearly jotting notes.

"Not sure, a few beers. Say, two pints?" he said.

"Anything else?"

"A bottle of wine, maybe over a weekend, no more than that, to be honest," he said.

"Very good. Very good," she said.

If Patricia had doubts, her voice hid them well.

"Now, may I ask, how much exercise do you take?" she asked.

"Just bought a bike," he lied.

"Great. A bicycle is good, very good – how many kilometres a day, a week?" she seemed enthusiastic.

"Roughly two, maybe three?" said Crowe. The lie felt comfortable now.

On and on. Very good. Very good. Questions 13 through to 25 nearly an hour on the line. Diet, relaxation, and meditation – Patricia suggested several useful meditation apps. Yes, she concluded after totting up the final score, he needed a one-to-one, she'd set the wheels in motion and she gave him the log-in details and password for the site he was currently scrolling through.

One-to-one. He really hoped it wasn't with deeply concerned Patricia.

Meditation – seriously?

Crowe rubbed his eyes. Turned off the phone. YOU ARE A VALUABLE PERSON. Bullshit.

He looked up at the clock, it was two in the afternoon. Crowe decided he needed a long walk. Get his bearings. Get out of the stagnant garret and get a feel for his surroundings. He located the lighter on the kitchen floor, shook the last of the fuel about and went to the window to light up. As he flicked the lighter he spied a movement in the courtyard.

It was that fox again. The one with the limp. It had appeared the morning before, snuffling and pulling on the bags when the Chinese had closed. It nosed around the takeaway's bins on a second sortie. The ears twitched as it hobbled, each step placed with a lurch, a dip, and the grunt of new exertion carried on the breeze.

A Kind of Drowning

The fields beyond the town offered a sanctuary to bolt for with just the main street to cross and then a long side street of shuttered shops. The piled up rubbish bags offered the young animal camouflage in the shadows.

Somewhere on the main street a dog barked. The narrow alley leading to the courtyard echoed the forlorn timbre. The fox froze. Every nerve and sinew alert. It raised its snout, searching about the air, hard-wired to the innate knowledge of the breed. Food could be poisoned. Not every dog was a fellow kindred, thought Crowe. After a pause, the fox snuffled around the bins and detritus.

Crowe fished the greasy chip bag out of the pedal bin. A few limp pieces and the gnarled hardened ends lay at the bottom coated in vinegar and cold grease. Opening the window slowly, he eased the bag onto the ledge and let it drop into the courtyard. It gyrated on the breeze before landing slowly onto the ground. The fox froze.

Crowe carefully pulled the curtains, until they created a narrow line of sight. Between the green drapes, Crowe could see the courtyard sliced by a line of sunlight. It danced on the fox's russet fur. Crowe held his breath watching. He made a kissing sound and the fox looked around and up at him. Crowe thought it could see his pallid face stitched to the unkempt moon-head skull peeking out through the dirty glass.

The animal's muzzle gave a toothy grin as it surveyed the open swirling bag. It then selected the chips with delicate bites. Through the curtains and the insulated glass, Crowe thought he could see a raw wound above the dew claw as it pressed down on the bag. Crowe fretted that the wound might become infected. The fox picking up on his thoughts, bent low and tenderly licked around the paw. It didn't yelp or whimper too much giving Crowe some hope.

A Kind of Drowning

"It does what it does, our '*Vulpes vulpes*'," said Crowe to the shadows of the room, "It eats birds, and weasels, and not forgetting voles. Merciless to less sturdier chicken coops, ruthless in murder,"

He thought it could hear his voice, it was looking around, crouching and alert. Satisfied there was no imminent danger, it selected the best morsels from the bag.

"You see, Mr. Fox, my life right now is like a wave," Crowe whispered, not wanting to spook it, "Like standing in the sea, waist-deep and a wave washes over you. Over your thighs, Fox. You get to your feet again, but the next wave hits you – here - chest height. You sort of stagger and then stand up, but the next wave, the next *bastardfucking* wave hits you in the face, washes you away. Lifts you off your feet. You feel like you're drowning…"

The fox arched a leisurely downward stretch, gave its wound another tender lick, smacked its lips, and in a heartbeat was gone.

It was the children that you never forgot. Nothing in your training prepares you for that. Dealing with little dead bodies.

They must have spent hours building their fort, the two boys. A dolmen fort made of haystacks. It had been hot, mid-summer, and the neatly folded T-shirt of one of them had somehow survived, badly singed. Crowe had been twenty-three when he stood in the incinerated remains of a field staring down at the melted toy pistols with the caws of carrion birds wheeling overhead. He was sweating in his uniform. It was the teeth, the pearly white teeth gleaming out through the burnt, raw looking flesh that haunted him. The two bodies huddled and welded together in the saturated straw. In the distance, the sounds of the sluggish hoses being packed away into the fire engines drifted on the wind. Eight years old he found out later, these two little souls. Despite himself, he found himself tenderly checking their pulses, his fingers pressed into roasted flesh. Of course there was nothing, but still…

He had vomited. Spewed up his breakfast onto his highly polished boots. It mixed in with the chemicals and foam and Crowe heaved more times until there was nothing left.

It had been a gorse fire that had got out of control, the ancient tradition that fanned by the wind had turned the surrounding lands into a tinder box, leaping across fields, burning everything in its path. Crowe had always hoped the smoke had killed them, not the fire. He tried to force out the thoughts of their last moments when they realised no one was coming to save them. No cavalry on the way. But he couldn't.

"*Ulex Europaes*, Gorse, fucking furze," he muttered, wiping the tears away with the heel of his left hand. He clenched it into a fist, ashamed. Where had this come from? He didn't know. It had risen deep within his chest, delivered in wracking gasps.

His father's solution, when he returned home that night was to break the seal on a bottle of Powers whiskey – *'Drink this it won't help, but it'll erase things for a while,'* he'd said. A Garda's life at times needed full erasure. A wiping of the memories that never went away.

Crowe took a deep breath. The tears burned. He turned away from the curtains, stared into the gloom and let the burning tears fall.

He cried for an hour. Then pulling open the curtains allowed the sunlight in. The sunlight was cathartic, and he needed to walk. To escape the slowly enclosing walls.

A Kind of Drowning

5

There were two universal truths for Crowe; a newspaper was never worth buying and the only real facts in one could be found between the pages of the sports columns. If you wanted to read a newspaper for free, there was always your friendly neighbourhood turf accountant; they kept longer hours than the library. And, if you wanted to catch a villain, you had to frequent his likely haunts. In his experience, most criminals were gamblers, both calculating and reckless; crime was a game and they always thought they were winners. Criminals like race horses had form and this Teflon D character was notorious for the sport of kings.

Being cut off suddenly from society had its freedoms. Shorn of responsibilities, past the derelict bank and shuttered up businesses, Crowe stepped into the bookies. The first thing he did was grab a handful of the small biros. It was a habit of his, on his days on active duty when those small plastic ball-points would be thrown into the side panel of the patrol car. You could never have enough pens.

He decided to scan the newspapers pinned to the shop's boards. It was late afternoon and the TVs blared their commentary to empty seats. He selected three meetings: each way on the favourites.

"A ten euro accumulator. The last race is 5:30," said the girl behind the glass.

"Feeling lucky today," replied Crowe handing his bet over. "Busy?" he asked.

"Dead," she replied as she handed him his slip.

"A coffee machine would help," said Crowe.

"Good luck with that," she said. Behind the glass her hair was as collapsed as her demeanour. She had the kind of features that could be anywhere between eighteen and forty, "That would involve the boss spending money. Moans about the recession," she continued.

Crowe suspected she was leafing through a magazine beneath the counter. It suited him; he had a sheaf of blank betting slips out of sight in his other hand.

"Would lend the place a little je ne sais quoi. Speaking of coffee, the new café in town, The Boogie Woogie? Who is the manager?" he asked.

"Melanie Fox," replied the girl.

Crowe wrote her name out on the back of the slip.

"Is she a hands-on-kind of boss?" he asked.

"Mel IS the *Boogie-Woogie*," replied the girl without looking up.

"What does she look like?"

"You'll know her the moment you see her."

"Thanks, one other question?" asked Crowe.

She looked up and around the room, he turned to see the same empty shop with the flatscreens alternating between odds, racing cards and horse races. The tacky looking carpet had stains, discarded takeaway cups, and used crumpled slips strewn across it.

Hardly Cheltenham, now is it? Townsend would've said.

"Other than me, I don't suppose you've had any new faces coming in recently? Perhaps over the last few weeks?" asked Crowe.

"Not much passing trade in this town. Just the locals," replied the girl.

Crowe could at last make out her name on her badge pinned to her waistcoat.

"Thanks, Karen," said Crowe.

Karen blew a chewing gum bubble. It burst loudly. She seemed to have stopped turning pages. Her expression had turned into a light bulb moment.

"We do get the odd new customer - a student type has come in recently. Haven't seen him before. Rides a mountain bike, brings it into the shop. Same type as my husband's."

"Does this student place his own bets or hand over a list?" asked Crowe.

"List. Mid to short odds, later race meetings, smaller cards. Sometimes he's in every day, sometimes once a week. Collects winnings close of business."

"Win often?"

Crowe found himself jotting down the details. He circled *'smaller cards'*, astute betting. An operator like Teflon D would need runners and couriers. A student type: he's a runner, thought Crowe. Punting by proxy. Maybe Quigley could shed more light.

"More often than not," she replied.

She seemed comfortable looking at him, her chewing and popping had gone up a gear.

"Do you text him when it's time to collect?" asked Crowe.

"Yes," she replied.

"Have you the number?"

"Are you the Guards?" she asked.

"No," he answered.

"Then no. Sorry," replied Karen. She started turning pages again, punctuated by gum pops. Worth a shot, he thought.

Crowe folded the slip with Mel Fox's name on it. Two foxes in one day, definitely a sign.

"Thanks, Karen, what time do you close?"

"Seven-thirty,"

Crowe walked out the door and ambled toward the Boogie-Woogie Café, looking out for expensive looking bicycles along the way.

The sun was dipping low across the sea, throwing pink and red hues across the clouds, and catching the crowns of the swell as it lapped against the harbour wall. At the corner, a woman was pulling the shutters down on the Boogie-Woogie Cafe. Dressed in a black leather biker's jacket with her unruly grey hair trussed in a bright yellow band, she was a compact looking woman. No question, it was Mel Fox.

Crowe lumbered toward her along the pavement. She stopped the shutter midway and watched him.

"Ms. Fox, I'm here about the kitchen porter position. Is it still open?" he gasped as he slowed down.

Mel Fox looked him over with one glance.

"Everyone calls me Mel," she said.

She looked like a charming combination of huckster, street-trader, and saint, packaged in black with white framed sunglasses sitting amid the wild curls like a tiara.

"Hello, Mel, my name is John Crowe."

Crowe leaned against the edge of the shutter frame. Maybe he was dazzling her with his wheezing, he wasn't sure.

"I know who you are, and the answer is no. I don't need that kind of baggage on my premises."

"Can I get a coffee at least?" he asked.

"Sorry, I'm closed." Said Mel.

Crowe thought long and hard. He straightened up and tugged his clothes together, he ran a hand across the top of his head, patting his wayward hair into place.

"Mel. I'll do the job for free and I can guarantee I'll show up every day. I only plan to stay in this town a week or two, I see it as a win-win."

"Can you come back tomorrow? I'd like to chat then. Good night," said Mel.

With a flick of her wrist, the shutter slid home and she snapped the lock shut.

"Derry Gallagher can vouch for me," said Crowe as she turned away.

"That's no guarantee of anything. Seven thirty tomorrow morning. See you then," said Mel over her shoulder.

Crowe watched her drive off in a battered looking green Hyundai. The breeze picked up as the twilight settled in. Crowe continued along the harbour wall, past the stacks of brightly coloured trays, lobster pots and seat boxes. Overhead, the sodium lights lit up the trawlers and the yachts bumping against the lines of tyres fixed to the wall. Crowe came to the edge of the jetty. The full force of the wind buffeted his fleece and his face felt the cold needles of sea spray. The temperature had dropped a few degrees forcing his hands into the pockets of his fleece. Inishcarrig glowed in the low sun, casting a long shadow across the sea.

A Kind of Drowning

Ten feet below his worn-out runners, the depths of the dark sea churned.

It would be so easy. Just stepping off. Let gravity do the rest. Jump and forget, let Alison and Cathal go on without him. End the online trolls, the hashtags, and the memes. Tweets going up like an incendiary kite with toxic threads on its tail. Give the closest to him some peace from the noise. #MadGardaScum Crowe couldn't swim, and he wouldn't resist, he'd keep his hands in his pockets…

His fingers clasped onto the phone. He pulled it out, maybe send a text. *'I'm sorry'*, or maybe phone, leave a voice message. He began to thumb a message to Alison and Cathal. A sudden tremor in his hand made him lose his grip and he watched in horror as the phone slipped from his grasp and dropped. He caught it. His hand and the elements fought for the phone. He watched in slow motion as it slid through his fingers.

Fuck me.

The phone glanced off the concrete edge and landed on one of the heavy tyres that protected the ships hulls. It began to yield to gravity, tilting slowly along the tyre. Crowe flattened himself onto the ground and reached out. Fearing his fingertips would tip it over into the depths, he made a lunge for it.

He retrieved it.

The screen had a faint mesh of new cracks and the message seemed to have been sent.

"Ohshitohfuckohjesuschrist…" he breathed.

Crowe looked around the world with a mix of shame and hopelessness for the last time. The brightly coloured trawlers boats were moored and unoccupied. Past them, the Boogie-Woogie was all shuttered up and dark. The roadway and jetty were deserted. The bleak twilight that enveloped Roscarrig wended its way to his knees. He turned back, facing towards the edge.

He wasn't sure if his foot had slid forward off the edge, but the sudden high plume of water to his right snapped him alert.

Had someone else jumped, or fallen, caught off guard by the wind?

Crowe hopped back a few paces. A shoulder high wall separated the stone jetty from a slipway for the RNLI lifeboat station. Standing on tip toes he peered over it. The playful bark of a dog drifted over the waves. The animal came out of the sea like a squat panzer tank; some breed of Staffordshire, a mean looking beast in a sturdy harness. Its owner, a shaven headed personification of the staffy was laughing. The dog's tail was wagging as its owner picked it up by the harness and tossed it back into the sea. It barrelled out of the water and shook itself on him. The man's laughter as he picked up the meaty dog and hugged it mixed with the excited licks and loud barks. The two leaned into the wind and trotted up the slipway, past the lifeboat station. Both had slavering grins. They didn't notice Crowe.

Another sound whipped around his ears. Squinting against the breeze, Crowe could hear a chainsaw buzz. For a brief moment, he thought it was scrambler bikes. A movement across the sea drew him to two small dots revving across the water toward the island. They disappeared over a wave.

Then they reappeared over the next crest. Two jet skis. In tight loops they came closer towards the harbour.

Crowe ran a sleeve across his eyes wiping away the tears and spray and remembered the bookies would be closed soon. He dashed down the jetty, loping in the same direction as the man and his barking sturdy pet.

The man had stopped, looking back at the jet skis. He made a gesture with his arm, Crowe barely noticed, maybe a familiar wave to them.

A Kind of Drowning

With a twist of acceleration, the two jet skis revved off in the direction of the island.

The Staffordshire panted in damp contentment; its unwavering gaze fixed on Crowe.

Dogs eat foxes, he thought. Cannibals. He was in a town full of fucking cannibals.

Cannibals riding mountain bikes.

Suddenly spooked, Crowe picked up the pace and began to sprint toward the safety of the town and its boiling pots of bones.

If he had been paying closer attention, he might have noticed the man was holding a walkie talkie.

6

TIK, TIK, TIK went the clippers until it felt like the phantom nail was trim. Some nerve endings never die, he thought as he woke from a troubled dream. The sheets were cloying to him in his night sweat. Crowe wondered what time the laundromat opened.

> `"..It is the opinion of the Garda Commissioner that this is the desirable course on review of the disciplinary hearing, and also after careful review of your service record to date and previous.."`

It was 4:30am. The official letter so carefully folded for weeks was now just ash. Its remains tipped into the pedal bin with most of last night's uneaten meal. The choice was simple; plug out of this crisis and survive or plug back in to THE BIG MACHINE and die. Crowe's listless sleep had been broken by the screeching of gulls. They had woken him from a dream of running through Roscarrig being pursued by cannibals with missing thumbs on bikes shouting and whooping his name. Sitting by the window, he'd hoped for the fox but the shrieking colony of gulls below was making an unholy racket. They made short work of the neatly tied and stacked black bags. His suicide text was stuck in drafts on his phone. Like a grenade with the pin pulled out, it could go at any time. He couldn't delete it. Or to be brutally honest, he didn't know how to.

After burning the letter, in a state of agitation he had stretched out on the floor, placed a pillow under his head and tapped play on the mediation app that Patricia recommended.

'Breathe in. Hold. Exhale; Breathe in. Hold. Exhale,' whispered the woman's voice. Chimes tinkled enticingly around her.

The gulls were now battling and scurrying across the roof beside the skylight. Crowe got up and closed it.

A Kind of Drowning

He tried again.

'*...Breathe in. Hold. Exhale.*'

The rumbling sound of an aircraft on this week's flight path, resounded around the garret. Crowe clenched his eyes and tried to breath and hold and exhale as the aircraft accelerated out over the sea. Trying to get to his peaceful place, he imagined himself sitting in a mounted AKAK gun shooting the bastard down.

The phone cut out without warning. He needed to charge it.

Fuck this, he thought.

He put on the kettle and lit a B&H from the hob. He'd need to buy a lighter at some point today.

Crowe shaved, carefully avoiding eye contact with the mirror and then with furtive glances at his reflection, made some attempt at combing his hair. Once it looked less of a mad man's arse, Crowe rummaged through the holdall and found a clean T-shirt. He felt a little fresher, then debated with himself on the twist of coke, snug in its little nook. He decided he didn't need that kind of perk up and scrambled together an instant coffee instead.

It was high tide as he walked along the coastline, the waves lapped over the barriers and bollards, the wash bubbled in the storm drains. Across the well-tended sports field, he sidestepped a flock of oyster catchers who eyed him and peeped inquisitively. The jetty was a hive of activity with the first of the catches landing. White vans nudged along to the point where he'd tried to jump.

The shutter was up in the Boogie-Woogie. He knocked on the door.

"On time, always a good start," said Mel.

She jabbed a thumb toward a table and two chairs.

A Kind of Drowning

The piece of paper on the table was printed out in **comic sans font**. If he ever came to power, Crowe would banish it for all time under pain of death. He remembered Alison emailed everything in comic sans. Considering their marriage, it was apt.

Duties / Requirements – *Keep all work surfaces and floors clean & sanitised. Sweep and mop floors. 'Can do' attitude in sweeping / mopping up messes to avoid hindering operations…*

He looked up at Mel. She was leafing through the VIP Magazine.

"Can do attitude?" he queried.

"Do you want the job or not?" she replied.

… *Arrange equipment and ingredient deliveries, take out rubbish and assist in food prep.*

He signed on the dotted line. He slid the sheet over, happy his hand hadn't spasmed. With her glasses sitting on her aquiline nose, her gaze was as steady and unblinking as a falcons.

"You'll get a split of the tips at the end of each week," she said.

"No need," replied Crowe, "I have some money put away,"

She closed the magazine. On the cover was Casey Clarke - *influencer*, social media blogger and *OMG* darling of the Red Tops. She posed with her new book *'Cooking with Casey Clarke'*.

"If I could have your attention, John?"

He looked up at Mel,

"You'll be on your feet for the whole shift. If I catch you with your feet up, you are out on your ear. There are kids working here, some with parents the same age as the man you put in intensive care," she continued, "If I see or hear of any attitude or aggression from you,

you are out on your ear. I have a good crew here; I don't need any problems."

Crowe nodded. He wasn't sure if he needed to salute, or just hug her.

"If everything goes according to plan, and you are still gracing us with your presence in two weeks' time, I'll look at putting you on the payroll,"

She rose and Crowe followed.

They passed the counter. Crowe noticed a pump sanitiser beside the cash register. Under the register, neatly stored were more of them,

"Expecting an apocalypse?" he asked.

"There's a certain demographic who frequent the Boogie-Woogie. You've been following the news?"

"I avoid the papers," replied Crowe.

"A type of H1N1 / SARS flu on its way, the retirement set love to see dispensers, you can never be too careful."

"It's spring? Isn't that a sort of winter phenomenon?" said Crowe.

"Never too careful, John, I have plans for this café, don't want the clientele keeling over." she changed the subject. "Do you play golf?" she asked over her shoulder,

"No," replied Crowe.

"Everyone should have a hobby,"

"So, I'm told," replied Crowe, "I take it you do?"

"Ladies captain at Roscarrig Golf Club, though I hate that term," she said, "It should be just captain. Its golf, GAA or nothing in this town. But that may all work in our favour. There's talk of the island, Inishcarrig, becoming a golf and leisure resort. Derry's involved. Do you know how much revenue the Ryder Cup generates?"

"No,"

"A cool one-hundred million revenue stream. Guaranteed."

"I've seen Derry's shirt cuffs, silver golf clubs and ball, stylish. He might need to update his wardrobe then."

"He's the club *'mens'* captain. He loves to boast he has a handicap of 2.8, but then so does Trump. That said, Derry speaks very highly of you. Too much if you ask me,"

Mel gave two pumps of the sanitiser at the end of the counter. Crowe gave a quick press. They turned right at the counter and into the prep area and grill. Compacted between two ovens and a sink stood the steel prep table. It was a very narrow space that led to a sharp L turn leading to the alleyway and bins.

"Deliveries come through the back. You will book in and log everything, store it and maintain it," she said, "You'll take full responsibility on this. If anything goes missing or damaged,"

"I'm out on my ear," said Crowe.

The shelves on either side were neatly stocked with various containers labelled in comic sans. Crowe noticed the CCTV over the door. There was another one on the other side of the door.

"What about foxes, urban ones?" asked Crowe.

"No foxes around here as far as I know," replied Mel.

"You'd be surprised," said Crowe.

"Hunting season ended last month. Farandore has an annual fox hunt; the second largest pack in Ireland is there," said Mel, "We got the spill over and had trays of sandwiches and coffee waiting. The mud was a nightmare to mop up,"

"I dodged a bullet so," replied Crowe.

"She was here, you know?" said Mel waving the magazine in her hand.

Crowe turned his head quizzically. Mel grinned,

"Casey Clarke, the one you were drooling over back there,"

"Her cookery programme is enlightening," said Crowe.

"My husband says the same. He still hasn't managed to make his way to the kitchen and cook her recipes though. She was in here with Ephraim Hunt,"

Crowe paused.

"Hunt? The property developer?"

"Same," she replied. She scrolled her phone and pulled up an image. Mel was wedged between stunning Casey and the gelled up tousled salt 'n vinegar head of Hunt. It was outdoors near the harbour wall. Hunt's *'What? Who me?'* expression was framed in his signature yellow tinted shades.

"They had coffee here, brought the town to a standstill. It was in VIP," she said.

"Don't read magazines, either" said Crowe.

Teflon D and Ephraim Hunt. Roscarrig was attracting the vultures. Cannibals and vultures conniving tooth and claw.

Mel reached for a pink apron hanging on a peg and tossed it to him,

A Kind of Drowning

"You can get cracking now," she said turning on her heel, "The cafe opens in half an hour. Mop and bucket are in the storage room. There'll be a delivery here at ten. Can you lift heavy weights?"

"No problem," he lied.

He now had a job, a roof over his head and last night's bet had come in. With another thousand euro in his pocket dolefully handed over by Karen, he could afford to splurge,

"I'll have a double espresso, Mel, three sugars, thanks."

He handed her a tenner,

"Keep the change," he said.

She handed it back,

"Get to work, John. You can take your break with Pavel and Maciej,"

"A shot of milk on the side?" he said.

But Mel was already in the café setting up for the day.

7

Thea Farrell hated to be late. Her mother, Grace brushed her hair, but Thea was impatient. She was excited. Grace hushed her with a gentle hand on her shoulder. Thea shouldn't get too excited; it would cause her to trip over her words. Get in a little muddle. Muddles were *silly billy*. It was Thea's first day of work, and she was keen to arrive on time. She kept turning her head to look at the radio clock on her bedside table.

Down Syndrome didn't deter her. She was nineteen years old and ready to make her mark on the world. The Boogie-Woogie Café would be the start. The words 'Boogie-Woogie' made her laugh. Thea's laugh was infectious.

> "There," said Grace, "Pretty as a rose,"

> "Rose of Tralee?" asked Thea. She was giddy with excitement.

> "Prettier," smiled Grace.

If Grace Farrell's insides were churning, it didn't show in her expression. Thea was acutely attuned to her parents' moods. Their communication happened over Thea's head when she was on YouTube, in mouthed words and choreographed eye-contact, but Grace's intuition told her Thea always knew what they were discussing. They had their misgivings about allowing Thea into a bustling environment. In fact, Andrew was dead set against it. But Grace held firm. He would come around eventually, she thought. She believed that Thea had to grow as a woman. Grace compartmentalised her fears and admired their gorgeous daughter. She was a gift. Everyone in Roscarrig knew Thea. Everyone loved her.

Thea's nose crinkled in a smile,

> "Don't worry – be happy, Mam," she said.

A Kind of Drowning

"I am, sweetheart, I am," said Grace.

She felt a twinge of empty nest; she fought the rising fears.

"Dad will drop you over," said Grace.

Andrew had been a knot of molten anger that morning, it was becoming a default setting these days,

"For Christ's sake – we're.. WE ARE running late," he shouted.

The staircase echoed his anger.

Andrew Farrell hated to be late – tardiness was the eighth deadly sin for him.

"Hey Dad. Don't worry," called down Thea.

Grace kissed the top of Thea's luxuriant soft hair,

"What would you like to do?" she asked

"I'll walk," replied Thea.

"She'll walk, Andy," shouted down Grace.

A volcanic silence simmered below on the stairs. Then they heard the sound of the van's keys being wrenched off the hook below the coat hanger.

Thea was dressed in the crisp white tee, blue jeans and comfortable pumps required for the cafe. Her hair was bundled up into her favourite pink scrunchy and she had put on her favourite friendship bracelets, gifts from her friends Lauren and Lucy at the café, along with her bright pink watch. They had promised to protect her, their solemn pledge to Grace.

Thea's backpack had her freshly laundered Garfield cat toy – he clung to the strap smugly. She put on her pink sunglasses and clipped her door key to her belt loop.

She waved goodbye to Andrew, who ignored her and over-revved his van out of the estate with his mobile pressed close to his ear. Thea walked down the narrow road from her home; a semi facing the sea. Some neighbours came out to wish her luck. With solid strides, Thea walked through the main street, and turned a sharp right to the harbour where The Boogie-Woogie and Mel waited.

She hugged Thea.

"Welcome, darling – ready for your first day?" said Mel.

Thea gave her best thumbs-up.

"Then let's get to work, Thea,"

"Let's get to work, Mel," said Thea.

Thea Farrell strode into the first day of her working life with a thumbs-up to everyone sitting in the café. They gave cheery thumbs-up back. It was the brightest corner in Roscarrig that day.

Thea shook the hands of the shift: Pavel and Maciej - the short-order cook and pastry chef. Cash-till and front-of-house were a moveable feast of half-bored teenagers, but Lauren and Lucy were regular. They made a big fuss of her.

Crowe was wrestling dishes out of the dishwasher. Forty eight hours into the kitchen porter gig hadn't improved his mood any.

"Don't worry, be happy," said Thea.

"I am happy, thanks," said Crowe.

"No, you're very grumpy," said Thea.

"This is my everyday happy face, and you are?"

"Thea. Thea Farrell. Pleased to meet you."

A Kind of Drowning

Crowe stacked the plates onto the workstation and wiping his hands in the soiled pink apron, he shook her hand,

"Nice to meet you. Now, I am *very* busy, Thea."

Thea tilted her head, the sunglasses now perched like Mel's. She narrowed her eyes reminding Crowe of a cat sizing up a sparrow.

"I am very busy too," she announced.

And left the kitchen to take the clientele's orders.

Lauren, the tattoo girl, sidled up to him, her expression was one long complaint,

"Be fucking nice to her, or I'll burst you, Crowe," she said.

"Yup. Be nice. Got it." replied Crowe.

Lauren tilted a plate off Crowe's wet pile, and it shattered on the kitchen tiles spectacularly.

"Be nice, Crowe. I know who you are and what you did to that man. We watch our own here. If you try anything, not only will I burst you, but Lucy will fucking burst you too - I'll fucking upload it too. Snapchat and TikTok you to fuck."

Lauren used profanities as punctuation behind the counter; *'fuck'* was practically a comma at peak time, offset with sullen silences and grunts at smoke break.

Lucy slalomed past the chefs with an armful of plates, her platinum bob pinned up in clips. She looked capable of dragging a trawler onto land by its anchor and was imbued with the same 'born too late' demeanour as Lauren. Both girls posed a credible threat to life and limb.

"Thanks, Lauren, I'll bear that in mind. Oh, and Lauren?"

Lauren whirled on her runners,

A Kind of Drowning

"Keep the language down around Thea," said Crowe.

Lauren raised a middle finger.

Mel made one of her sudden apparitions,

"Next breakage will be out of your wages, John," she said with one eye fixed on the tables outside, hoping the exchanges didn't drift. She enforced a *Bad Behaviour* jar of €1 for charity. Lauren was the gift that kept on giving.

"Doing this for free, remember? Mel," said Crowe.

"I'll take it out of your tips then,"

That'd break the bank, he thought.

Crowe stacked the pile away and swept up the shards of crockery. His shirt was clinging to him, long rivulets of sweat were pooling around his lower back and running down the crack of his arse.

"And you need to work on your personal freshness, I can smell the whiskey from here, Crowe. Do you *actually brush* your teeth?"

Volunteering was now becoming a Dante-esque level of torment.

Crowe sorted the dishes and packed Lucy's massive haul into the dishwasher. Pavel throwing the pots into the sink like javelins spilled suds over Crowe and the tiled floor, turning it into a skating rink that needed regular mopping.

He would give it another week.

Thea had her first orders in. Crowe looked up and saw the radiant glow of achievement in Thea's smile. Sunshine on legs. He sought the darkened corners of the kitchen, slipping out into the wheelie-bin lined alley for an unscheduled smoke break.

He didn't feel worthy of such a glow.

He scrolled down his smart phone; twenty messages sent to Alison and Cathal without response. Identifying himself as 'Podge' and Dad didn't seem to help. His old phone had all the photographs, dead in the drawer of THE BIG MACHINE in Dublin's Phoenix Park HQ. His new one had four numbers on the speed dial – Alison, Cathal, Mel Fox and Derry Gallagher. Don't worry, be happy. He pressed his head against the wall and dragged the B&H until a loping arc of ash fell off the butt.

Fuck that, he thought.

He crushed the butt into the ground and wiped his sweaty brow with the apron. He had another four hours to go before a date with his bottle of Jameson, to wash down the snack box from The Dragon Inn.

8

It was a Monday afternoon when Crowe met Clodagh Robertson. Mondays and Tuesdays were his days off. The library was an old schoolhouse restored back to its former glory. A blocky Church of Ireland edifice, the stones, laid in Victorian austerity, gave it a solid sense of purpose. From across the carpark, he watched Clodagh freewheel in on an old fashioned bicycle with a basket on its bars. She was wearing dark skinny jeans, a loose striped top, and a vivid yellow rain jacket with reflective stripes. Expensive like her Nikes. Crowe looked at his wrist and remembered he didn't have a watch. She clicked past him to the door of the library and expertly wrangled the bike against the wall. One of Roscarrig's sudden onshore breezes hoisted the rain jacket hood over her head, masking her voice,

"Sorry, could you repeat that?" asked Crowe.

"I won't be a minute," said Clodagh.

"I have all day," replied Crowe.

Clodagh locked the bike, squatting lithely. Crowe found something else to focus on other than her long legs and deft fingers. She wrestled the jacket's hood back against the wind and he got a glimpse of shoulder-length hair, a long nose, but not disproportionate to her features, a stubborn chin, a mouth set in concentration and small eyes. Every part of her seemed to be measured and focussed.

Crowe allowed her a few moments to open the doors, deactivate the alarm and switch on the overhead fluorescents.

The interior really needed candles to finish the effect, he thought.

It was only his second time ever in a library. Alison had read all the books to Cathal at night, she belonged to the local library's book club. The more Crowe thought about Alison, the more he realised that she was the kind of woman who seemed to think the planet would stop turning if she did. If her life were stopped at any point in a freeze-frame, Alison would be captured doing something 'important'. Everything Alison did was 'important'.

Including the Hospital Consultant.

He toyed with the old library card fished out of his battered wallet. It's only company was his bank card, €20.00 and his driver's licence.

"How may I help you?" asked Clodagh.

"My card won't update on the Library website?" replied Crowe.

Standing at the opposite side of the desk that ran the length of the library he felt like he was shouting over a stockade.

Clodagh took the library card from Crowe. She tapped her keyboard. An industrial sized box of rubber bands, a stock of paperbacks and a lethal-looking stapler were nudged aside to allow elbow room. The word 'gauche' sprung to mind; the Librarian occupied more space than was allowed,

"I'll need your address please?" said Clodagh.

"Sundrive Ave, Flat 3, Roscarrig Main Street," he replied.

"Have you a recent utilities bill or confirmation of this address?" she asked

"I've just moved here. Gallagher Estates are the letting agent,"

"I know Derry, so I don't think that'll be a problem. Done. All updated,"

She handed back the card. Crowe noticed she hadn't an engagement or wedding band.

"My son says that I seem to have an aura around tech. It doesn't like me," said Crowe.

A Kind of Drowning

He found everything these days an immense challenge – cash transactions, shopping lists, washing up and cleaning. It was as if the reboot in his skull was caught in a loop.

"Scan your card first and then the book's barcode. On the back there,"

"I know what a barcode looks like," said Crowe.

As he ambled around the shelves, Crowe found himself looking at her. Through furtive aisles between the shelves, he watched her movements. She looked like a city girl who through bad luck had wound up here. A star too bright for this backwater. Crowe brushed against a shelf and dislodged a volume. It dropped onto the aged wooden floor with a resounding boom.

'fuck'. The expletive drifted across the library's beams. Then with the gait of a fossilised T-Rex, Crowe disappeared amid the shelves.

Two old ladies clanged open the library's doors and frog-marched themselves in with shopping bags full of returns. They waved at Clodagh who coldly smiled back.

Crowe scanned the shelves, the spines offered very little by way of identification. Block red fonts caught his eye, but he had no idea about the authors. A-Z, he worked backwards and forwards. He had no idea what he was doing. This began a spiral of unexpected anxiety. Occasionally in the maze, he'd meet the two septuagenarians. They stood their ground, not giving an inch if he had to squeeze past them. He caught some of their mutterings that hung in their hair like the virulent miasma of an old woman's kitchen,

"I see it's that Robertson one… back at home again… terrible; husband threw her out – the drink you know…Just like the mother – couldn't keep a man…"

A Kind of Drowning

He spotted Clodagh taking a book from the returns shelf and walking towards him.

"I'm sorry to ask, but can you recommend something?" he asked.

Clodagh stared at him,

"Have you a genre in mind?" she asked.

"Not sure," replied Crowe.

"What do you like to read?"

"Nothing too demanding?"

"Nothing too demanding might be sports, sports biography? Shelves just behind you."

She seemed keen to get on with things. An innate impatience with the general pace of life hung around her.

"I like a good adventure; a page turner," said Crowe.

It sounded hackneyed and Clodagh's expression said it too. He imagined her mind mouthing page-turner, filed beside 'unputdownable'.

"Well…, the author's names might help. Child, Forsyth, Maclean, Patterson…? If its classical, Dickens, Wells, Conan Doyle, Childers, Melville… We have a great selection of Irish writers, contemporary, though you don't strike me as romantic fiction."

Hilarious, thought Crowe.

She side-stepped between the shelves and disappeared. Out of desperation, Crowe decided 'C' was the best guess. He trailed around behind her.

She was already gone. He crouched low scanning the lower shelves, he spied a Cornwell, some forensic thriller. He thumbed the pages but felt the font was too big. Is this what retirement felt like? He picked a dog-eared Lee Child and ambled over to the dangerous machine. He scanned the book out without setting all the alarms off and spun on his heel,

"Appreciate your help, thanks," he said to Clodagh.

She looked up and nodded absently.

Crowe shuffled out of the library, clinging to the book under his arm.

9

Elvis Presley was playing in the background. He was wondering if you were lonesome tonight. Mel had the café's radio tuned to a golden oldies station. Crowe thought about the Elvis festival the Garda station had held on his first posting. It had been a Garda charity event for the local hospice. Quigley had belted out *'Suspicious Minds'* and Crowe had met Alison for the first time. Alison loved Elvis. Quigley and Alison counterweights to his life right now.

Crowe was more of a baroque man, Glen Gould, and Bach.

Pavel and Maciej were a secretive Polish pod that spoke and interacted with each other to the point Crowe couldn't tell them apart. They both had their earphones on, Pavel's head bopping to some death metal bombardment. Maciej was scrolling his phone between bites of the lunch they had prepared for the crew – omelette, chips, and salad. Crowe had gleaned on their days off they serviced cars for cash in the driveway and mended walls, fences and on occasion, painted houses inside and out. He suspected their English was better than they were letting on. The art of conversation is dying, he thought.

Thea looked over at Crowe,

"What are you reading, Mr. Grumpy?" she asked.

Crowe had forced a space in the kitchen where they could sit. He scrolled down Quigley's reply fragmented across the screen: *Teflon D lying low in R/Carrig. But NO close protection – orders from top brass. Q.*

"An adventure, Thea, all about cops and robbers. You?"

He thought about the Jet skis he had seen. He texted: *are the sons out here too?*

Quigley responded – *yep*.

Crowe Googled *Jet Skis and Fast Power Boat bye-laws'*. He pulled his sheaf of betting slips,

"Got a pencil? Pen?" he asked Thea.

Without looking up she took her biro out of her scrunchy and handed it to him. He jotted down some facts on the back of them. He handed the pen back, she slotted it into her scrunchy. One of Lauren's tells.

Thea folded out Mel's latest VIP magazine.

"I like celebrities, I love Casey Clarke," she said, *"Cooking with Casey Clarke – JUST SIMPLE!"*

It was a good impersonation.

Crowe slid Quigley's message closed and turned the magazine towards him. It was a nightclub somewhere in Dublin. Casey kissing Hunt, the kiss loaded for the camera phones around them. A match made in bloggerverse heaven,

"She's very pretty," replied Crowe.

Lauren passed by and looked over his shoulder,

"Ephraim Hunt, don't like him. Fucking cokehead. Chasing young girls. A nonce."

She took the magazine,

"It's Thea's," said Crowe.

"It's mine," said Thea,

"Says there that Casey is twenty two?" said Crowe.

"Twenty two, Lauren," intoned Thea.

"Well, he looks about sixty. Your age, old man," said Lauren,

"Says here, he's thirty eight?" said Thea. She circled a neat finger nail around the caption under the picture.

"C will do that to you, Thea. Nonce. Him, not you, Crowe. The nonce snorts two tramlines through a Ben Franklin, yeah? That's a $100-dollar bill, yeah? All the time. Thea's dad legit told me."

Crowe flashed a glance at Thea. He saw a momentary unease.

"How would he know that?" asked Crowe taking the magazine off Lauren carefully.

He handed it over to Thea.

"He told me. He was laying floors last year. Saw him do it. Right in front of everyone, doesn't give a fuck," said Lauren, "those stupid yellow sunglasses he wears supposed to be photophobia, yeah? Real reason coked to fuck twenty-four seven. Truth,"

Thea blushed.

"You missed your calling, Lauren. You should be writing for this rag," said Crowe.

"It's not a rag," said Thea.

She spread the magazine out and splayed her fingers, pressing down the edges and returned to her read.

Lauren, suddenly frozen out by Crowe and Thea reading, hovered, then headed out to the tables.

"Lauren's funny," announced Thea, "I am going to a party with her this weekend. A school reunion."

She reached for a packet of crisps and gave the bag a squeeze. An impish grin followed when the top opened with a loud pop. Pavel and Maciej looked up as if the gag were already old.

A Kind of Drowning

She offered the open bag to Crowe.

"That's one word for her," he said. Though it was the first time the spider tattoo had stopped moving, "will she watch out for you?"

Thea opened out the bag, laying it flat between them and they shared the crisps. Crowe prised the spare bread roll apart and packed it full of them.

"Of course, silly billy. I know her since I was five," said Thea without looking up, "It is in the GAA club. She is going to do my hair."

"Thea, do you know how to delete a message on a phone in drafts?" he asked.

Without looking away from the article. She took Crowe's phone, glanced up and tapped the screen.

"Here you go," she said, "You need a screen protector,"

The suicide text was now just binary dust.

"Thank you," he breathed.

It was just after the lunchtime rush had abated, tables were cleared, the sink was piled up and the café was gearing up for the early bird. Lauren and Lucy had skulked past to grab a quick smoke in the alley. Pavel and Maciej were in the alley too, taking an unscheduled smoke break. Mel had left to run an errand, leaving the crew unsupervised.

Crowe hadn't been aware of anything at first as he sluiced the pots and pans, but raised voices drifted into the kitchen.

MONGOLOID. It echoed. Crowe stopped. The chant was repeated, the voices young and harsh.

Before he could think it through, Crowe was out of the kitchen and into the café.

A Kind of Drowning

Thea was shaking and crying, her shoulders heaving. Three men who were old enough to know better were pointing at a broken pile of ice cream, drinks, and glass,

"You *fuckin'* retard! Watch what you're doing, you dummy." yelled one man. He was in a hoodie, "What sort of place employs a freak?"

"Mon-gol-oid, she's mon-gol-oid," sang the other hoodie. He sported a fade haircut, virtually shaved pink at the back and sides. A gelled mane swirled upwards like icing sugar.

Three pups, Quigley would have called them. Where the hell was Lauren? He needed her and Lucy. Lucy would scare the shit out of Satan himself.

Crowe thought about running to the alley for the girls. Three against one. Tight odds even if the yahoos remained sitting.

"It's okay, Thea," said Crowe, "You go back and find Lauren. I'll clean this up."

She turned and dashed to the kitchen, wracked with sobs.

"It has a *name*? The mong has a name?" laughed Fade. He flicked his attention to Crowe. "You're a sad fat bastard in the pink apron," he sneered, "You fucking her, fat boy?"

"Might be time to finish up, lads," said Crowe.

He looked around the café, one table was occupied, an elderly couple studiously ignoring the scene.

No help.

"We ordered three ice-creams, special needs here fucking dropped them," said Fade.

"Her name is Thea," said Crowe.

A Kind of Drowning

"Thea fucktard," said Mr. Hoodie. He was big, built on take-aways, crisps and litres of carbonated sugar. His gaze was unwavering, cold, calculating.

"Thea fucktard mongoloid," he said.

"Mon. Go. Loid," Fade mouthed. He made lapping gestures with his tongue.

"Right lads, that's enough," said Crowe.

It was the third one at the table that Crowe was worried about. The one that hadn't said a word but took everything in. He was thin, rat-like. The big bastards, after a truncheon to the gut, would fold up and cry. It was the small ones you had to worry about. A little fucker like this one, beaten down from the day he was born, wouldn't go down as easy.

He'd make a fight of it.

"Take your order elsewhere, gents, if you please," said Crowe.

"Or?" challenged fat hoodie.

"Or I'll have to ask you to leave," said Crowe.

"In a pink fucking apron?" said Fade.

"It'll be red in a few moments, son. Now I'm afraid, gentlemen, I'll have to insist." said Crowe. He'd pitched his voice to a tone lower.

Great, he thought, now I'm Batman.

"You can take our order, just no mongs near the table, yeah? No retarded slow cunts," Ratty had decided to speak.

"No slow people," chimed hoodie number one.

"Sorry, lads, the kitchen's closed. Get your 99's or whatever you ordered somewhere else."

A Kind of Drowning

The three stood up simultaneously.

Crowe took a single step back,

"Let's all leave nicely now," said Crowe.

He scanned the table. No mobiles. Nothing to film. He looked around. No one was watching. The elderly couple were bent into a newspaper. Crowe studied the floor, the creeping ice cream, amid the shattered glass.

"Go fuck yourself, you fat cunt," said hoodie number one.

Crowe's movements were instinctive. He delivered a kick to hoodie's knee that collapsed him onto the glass and melted sundae. Hoodie writhed and cried out. Some glass had entered his leg. One shard stuck out like a bloodied finger. Crowe bent down and hoisting him up by the hood, ensured on the way back up his skull connected with the face of Fade 2. Fade 2's nose exploded, streaming blood down his wispy moustache. Crowe dropped Hoodie back onto the floor and delivered a swift toe poke into his face.

Two noses shattered. Not bad.

Ratty immediately backed away. But only a few inches. Crowe couldn't see what he was holding in the right hand.

"Sorry about that, the floor's a little slippy," said Crowe, "That'll be €20, lads."

"Fhuk-uuff!" roared Fade. His face was a mask of red as he tried to wipe away the blood with a napkin. Hoodie held his hands up, trying to protect his face from the next incoming kick.

Crowe shoved Fade 2 onto the chair and Fade sprawled under the collapsed wood of the chair.

"€30, lads," said Crowe.

A Kind of Drowning

Ratty's face was a ripple of calculations. He slid into his back pocket whatever he had been holding and fishing around in his skinny jeans, found and threw a €50 onto the table,

"Call it quits?" he said.

His voice was even, unemotional, measured. Crowe's instinct was right; he was looking at the puppet master.

Mel pulled up outside in her Hyundai, spied what was going on and barged through the front door.

"There's CC TV here. We will take your images and send them around every café in the area. Every café, every bar, every Garda station and post them up on our FB page and Instagram," she said.

The three pups hobbled out. The two diners continued as if nothing had happened and Crowe went looking for the bucket and mop.

"That chair is coming out of your tips," said Mel.

Crowe strode past her without a word.

He found Thea in the kitchen. Lauren was holding her, rocking her. She glanced at Crowe with something close to grudging respect.

"She ok?" asked Crowe.

Lauren nodded.

"Don't post that up, Lauren" he said as he hauled out the mop and bucket, "I don't need the extra publicity,"

"Didn't see a thing, Crowe,"

"Thanks," said Crowe.

"Crowe?" said Lauren.

"Yeah?"

"That was fucking deadly."

"Let's hope they don't come back," said Crowe.

He mopped up the mess and swept up the glass. He glowered at the couple when one remarked,

"I blame the parents. Pushing that poor girl. She should be at home. That mother Grace is always pushing her. They make me uncomfortable, those type. They call them special ones these days."

The woman who uttered it stirred her tea imperiously. Her companion, the man said nothing. They were well scrubbed retirees emanating smugness. Crowe adjusted his bulk toward them and farted long and slowly.

"Here's my special one," he muttered.

His emission did the trick.

"Well done," said Mel dashing for the door, "You've managed to drive out every bloody customer," she fanned the door back and forth trying to expel Crowe's waft.

"You can take it out of my tips, Mel." he replied.

"You're fired, Crowe. I can't have you whaling in on my customers."

Mel's swings were getting more vigorous,

"Christ, Crowe what did you eat?"

"I was quitting anyway, Mel," replied Crowe over his shoulder as he skulked back to the kitchen. Down past Pavel and past Maciej kneading a great block of dough. Past Lauren who shook his hand, past Lucy who managed the briefest of nods, her big arms folded. Crowe stopped at Thea. He held her close to his bulk and whispered,

"Don't worry, be happy,"

And then out into the darkened alley where he unfastened his greasy, bloodied apron and dumped it in the bin.

The alley cut out onto the seafront. A modified Honda with stripes and a spoiler ripped up the road unevenly. Crowe could make out the bloodied faces of the trio as it passed, all grinding gears and vibrating exhausts.

Never a guard around when you need one, he thought.

As he trudged up the street, some sixth sense told him that there would be something for him in the post box. Some umbilical tendril to the BIG MACHINE was still hard-wired into his psyche like an infection. The BIG MACHINE never accepted failure or rather failure it couldn't hide, deny, cover up or redirect to some far-flung rural station. Remembering what happened the day before, Crowe had looped the apartment key through an old shoelace. A makeshift key ring. He wouldn't be startling the Polish family on the floor below today.

Crowe had forgotten the apartment number. His inner peace was unbalanced, and his gut was in turmoil. He ran a bloodied finger down the lines of names on the letterboxes until he guessed the one without a name was his. Opening it, he pulled the official brown envelope out with his old work address crossed out. He sensed it had boomeranged around Dublin before reaching him judging by the biro, and he was mildly insulted not to have had a courier hand it to him for sign off.

He took a breath and opened it.

It was a temporary domestic violence restraining order from Alison; reason: unwelcome and unwarranted text messages from a phone other than his registered on their pay plan. 'causing considerable distress.'

A Kind of Drowning

Crowe didn't remember slamming the postal box or punching it repeatedly until a voice in the corridor above told him in Easter European English to *"Shut'd-d'fhuck Up!"*

Crowe kept slamming anyway.

10

"Who are you, Pius John Crowe?"

The long sweeping stretch of beach was five minutes' walk from his garret. The dawn was reaching farther back into the night and every morning come what may, Crowe's walks allowed him to switch off his misfiring mind before his shift. Only he'd been fired yesterday. He felt bad about leaving Thea, he had enjoyed her uncomplicated companionship during their breaks. He was fearful she would change, become hard and bitter like Lauren or completely indifferent like Lucy. He fretted she'd walk by without acknowledging him. Crowe realised he was utterly alone.

Quigley had stopped responding – the last text from him said simply: *SICK.*

Doors were suddenly closing on him. The lifeboats were taking on water.

Inishcarrig loomed across the bay. Sheer cliffs on one side spewed plumes of white back into the sea. Crowe kicked off his running shoes and stuffed his socks into them. Tying the laces together, he draped the runners around his neck. He sank his toes into the cold ebb tide, allowing the sand ooze in between his toes. Shutting his eyes, he let out a roar, a howl of pent-up fury. It came from deep within him. The wind snatched the cry and hurled it around the deserted beach. He screamed and roared at the top of his lungs until he was coughing up phlegm. He vomited up his latest hangover and wiped his beard with the sleeve of his fleece. He cupped some seawater and sloshed it around his gums. He spat it out and savoured the aeons old taste of salt.

A sudden shredding of the sky made him look up. A helicopter clattered across the bay from the mainland toward Inishcarrig. He stopped and lit a cigarette watching it. Banking sharply, it disappeared behind the Martello tower. It rose briefly with a slow 180 degree turn and settled just out of sight. Crowe paused. He lit his next from the butt of the last and let the smoke drift about him. Maybe it was the streamlined power of the machine or its anti-social arrival, that started a small, distant early warning system somewhere amid his synapses. The engine dying down echoed across the channel; a pulsing *whu-whump-whu-whump* wheeze.

Checking his phone, the time read 5:55am.

Crowe pulled on his socks and shoes and started walking along the beach. Coming to the bend of the sand that led to the estuary, he saw a yellow kayak powered by someone in a very orange helmet. With strong sweeps, they pulled through the tide and disappeared from view. A sudden increase in engine noise made Crowe look over his shoulder. The helicopter rose from the island, began a lazy sweep around it and then with a powerful scream it clattered off towards the mainland like a sleek hornet.

It had been on the island for nearly an hour. Maybe it was the elusive Canadian Billionaire, Norcott arriving incognito, but to coin a phrase from Quigley; it didn't *"pass the smell test"*.

One person might know.

Derry Gallagher.

***

If Gallagher was holding a busted flush, he was doing his very best to bluff with smooth casino cool,

"If a helicopter landed there, I'd have got the heads-up, John. I'm in the loop on that." he said. "I've ensured Mr. Norcott has my contact details,"

To emphasise, he nodded to his highly polished, though inactive desk phone. If anything, it underlined his disappointment.

"Hardly a FOR SALE sign on the island now, is there? Just saying what I saw," said Crowe.

He looked at the calendar over Gallagher's shoulder. It was the last week of April.

May, June, July.

"I'd like to extend the lease. I'll pay cash. Right now. Covers me 'till end of August?" said Crowe.

"That would certainly do it." Gallagher grinned,

"Take it out of the money belt," said Crowe.

"Are you okay, John? You look a little off,"

"Never better, Derry. So, this helicopter; any ideas?" asked Crowe.

"I'll have to get back to you on that," said Gallagher.

"Is this Norcott the sort of guy who lands unannounced?" said Crowe.

He wondered when the elusive Hilary showed up for work. Her desk was studiously clean and deserted.

"Definitely landed?" asked Gallagher over the rim of his glasses, "Not Air-Sea Rescue? Big red and white helicopter? Sometimes they do practice exercises, taking off, circling, and landing,"

"It was a small black one. I wasn't paying that much attention. Saw it take off and go around Inishcarrig once. I took a photo,"

Crowe showed Gallagher the image on his phone.

"Not Air/Sea Rescue, though it's very blurry," agreed Gallagher.

"And you knew nothing about it?"

Gallagher stared at Crowe's phone like a husband shown proof of his wife's infidelity by a PI.

"No," he said.

"I'd worry about that if I were you."

Gallagher seemed temporarily lost. Crowe wanted to press, but where does duty, such as it was, end, and recuperation begin?

"I'll leave the bedding out Friday?" he said

"Yes, yes… of course, John. Of course," replied Gallagher.

Crowe spied the coffee machine and crushed out a double lungo. He took a cup with him,

"I'll drop it back at Christmas," he said knowing Gallagher's mind was elsewhere.

Gallagher barely nodded, transfixed by the laptop's display.

With no job and the new project of a villain to pursue, Crowe walked toward the edge of the town. He stood at the T junction that led eventually to the motorway; Dublin 50km / Belfast 105km. A faded looking aircraft indicated the airport. Like the town, the sign was rusted and covered in seagull shit. No-one would willingly venture out here, unless they were broke, desperate, or waiting for the housing crisis to abate. Turning on his heel, Crowe's route took him past rows of glasshouses and farmyards where rusted implements became trellises for ivy and weeds. The roads were narrow, no more that boreens, with long lines of wild grass growing up through the middle.

He was hoping for his fox and imagined that it was lying amid the late spring growth, the tall grasses and wild spring flowers, watching him.

He'd order an extra bag of chips tonight and leave some in the courtyard for it.

Sensing he had reached a dead end, he doubled back toward the main street and decided to walk the half mile to the old churchyard and the newer builds.

Looking for the lair of the gangster with a missing thumb.

11

Sometimes Thea slipped out of the house without telling her parents. She knew that it was wrong. Once the whole town had gone looking for her and Grace, driven by gut instinct, had found Thea sitting on one of the dunes staring out to sea. Sometimes her parents' rows would escalate past heated whispers or staring competitions. Tonight, was one of them. Yelling. Angry yelling. Thea had rocked back and forth on her bed, hands over her ears. The shrieks from Mam were becoming too much.

"Don't worry, be happy," Thea mantra'd.

She'd put on her headphones, scrolling Spotify until she found her happy mix. It wasn't enough. She was still shaking from the big bullies in the cafe. Thea had been scared by them. Mr Grumpy had stood up for her. She liked Mr. Grumpy. Even if he was always grumpy. A full moon beamed into her bedroom. Beyond the window it backlit the sea and the island. A Roscarrig native, she knew the tides, knew the secret places and trails of the other children. Sometimes she had followed them, curious, eager to join in their play. Sometimes they threw sand and pebbles at her, chasing her off. Other times, they just teased or ignored her. But she was always curious. Everything interested her and everything scared her at the same time. Thea loved the sea. Loved dangling her legs off the island's cliff face staring up at the moon on nights like this. Thea loved the moon.

In the morning, it would be all kisses and cuddles, but Thea sensed, no, Thea *knew* things weren't happy with her parents. Shouting at each other. Mum behaving like a bully, calling dad silly names; her mouth pinched up and lined as she spoke. The more Thea dwelt on this the more her music was just white noise and the more she became unsettled.

A Kind of Drowning

Something crashed below. Followed by the tinkling of shattered glass. Thea decided: She was going for a walk.

The first whispers of a warm summer came in through the window, catching her curtains with the sailing boat motifs. Thea pulled out her white Minnie Mouse hoodie and tugged it on. She stuck her head out the window and looked along the line of back gardens fenced in wooden panelling. A few lights beamed out. Beyond, long fields squared off by hedgerows led down to the beach. Dad thought that more houses would be built soon. He hoped it would because he could get more work for his business.

    "Maybe next year will be better," was something he said every morning.

But more houses would then block out the view of the island. Thea didn't want that.

The argument must have been coming from the kitchen. Thea heard a window slam shut, reducing the shrill din and Dad's loud roars.

She unplugged her phone and tip toed down the stairs. She took her keys, put on her reflective arm band, and closed the door behind her. Taking the well-worn sandy pathway behind the houses that bisected the fields like a permanent scar, Thea Farrell headed toward the beach.

She might even see some seals along the way. They reminded Thea of dogs.

It was 11:15pm.

12

The Twitter post got over a thousand retweets in less than ten minutes. Thea's impish grin viralled across time zones from the Canadian west coast to the outer islands of New Zealand. Missing. Please RT. A Facebook page was set up, that too began flashing across feeds around the globe. The TV, the radio, Thea became the hot topic around canteen tables with tabloids folded out. Open plan offices became conspiracy soapboxes with grisly conclusions and outcomes. Night shift cleaners folded her away and threw her face into black bin sacks. Over the week, social media interactions climbed into a million. Celebrities and radio hacks joined in. Fishermen ploughed the channel between the island and the mainland; search teams of volunteers assembled in early morning light: Roscarrig was finally on the map.

But Thea was in the wind.

She was gone.

Then, in the dawn light of the tenth day, a call came in from one of the search boats. A body had been found. A crowd had gathered at the harbour waiting for the trawler. Thea was returned to her home town not three hundred yards from the doorstep of the Boogie Woogie Café. She was then removed by hearse to the Coroner. Crowe hadn't been there, he had been out walking along the headland, scanning the rocks and piles of seaweed working off a whiskey hangover. But Derry Gallagher had been on the quayside. He'd filled Crowe in. He thought Thea's father had looked *'relieved, if you understand my meaning'*, but then, what parent wouldn't, waiting for a child to come home, alive, or dead.

The narrative shifted on the social media feeds. Thoughts and prayers, candles, emojis of hugging, hearts, and tears. #RIPTHEA. Mel had tweeted her staff would wear pink for the funeral. The community replied everyone would wear a 'bit of pink'.

A Kind of Drowning

Crowe shook the last of the aerosol hair dye and gave it a final squeeze. Staring back was a haggard, lined horror show with cropped, unkempt hair, now a shade of 'Daring Bubblegum'. Not that he had a lot to dye; the roots were in poor flaky shape and he had no idea what the back would be like. The smell of chemicals reminded him of Alison, the incense of everyday beauty maintenance. Like the lipstick she never went outdoors without. Like the smell of nail varnish remover. He washed the morning's search off his hands, working the soap through his fingers smelling of kelp. The private quest for Thea was over, the pulling kelp apart on his path, as if each mound could have been a body. His hands had developed tremors after he had heard of Thea's death. The soaping became more furious. His hands became a blur of suds and when he stopped his ablutions and looked up; he was crying.

The tears of a clown.

Thea wasn't much older than Cathal.

The twist of coke sitting snug under the toilet S-bend whispered to him. He fished the pink-dappled marigold gloves out of the pedal bin. He dashed back to the toilet, his synapses firing in anticipation. Reaching under the S-Bend, he freed the packet and held it up...

He threw it in the toilet and flushed. The coke bobbed about in defiance. Crowe flushed it again. It floated in *fuck-you* circles.

Maybe another time, he thought as he fished it out. He wiped it down, checked for leakage into the packet and satisfied the product was untouched, returned it to its nook.

A cigarette and instant coffee would have to suffice.

Crowe stumbled out of the bathroom; a sudden compunction gripped him. He needed to hear Cathal's voice – even a grunted *'Fuck-off'* would have brought him deep joy. He needed to hear his child's voice. He needed to hug his son and ruffle his hair which always annoyed him.

Fuck the restraining order.

Crowe's hands were greasy with soap, the phone slid about like an eel, stubbornly evading his grip. He went straight to voice mail; 'leave a message', Cathal's voice had lost its boyishness, the threshold of a man.

"It's Dad. I love you. Call me some time, I'd love to hear from you," was all Crowe could mutter.

The phone slipped from his fingers and bounced on the wood flooring. Crowe palmed away tears with the heel of his hand. Every morning, Thea had said to him "Don't worry, be happy, Mr Grumpy."

Now that greeting was forever silenced, engulfed by the unforgiving depths.

"The father had seemed relieved". Derry Gallagher had touched a finger against his pitted nostril when he had said this. A lifetime of small-town dirty secrets had flashed across his features in his all too easy smile.

Twenty years of policework, bloodwork, arrests, convictions, and slimy little pups getting away with it began to tap Crowe on the shoulder. It had come out of nowhere. That cop voice that says, 'Knowing is one thing, proving it is another."

The father had *seemed* relieved. Thea was a strong young woman, thought Crowe, Thea could deal with most situations; she didn't seem the drowning kind.

Crowe reassembled himself on the carpet. Dripping soap, he picked up the phone and with his stubby thumbs, punched in the one number he knew better than Alison's: Olivia Cutts, the Assistant State Pathologist.

13

There is something inherently wrong when a funeral is attended by the young, thought Crowe. Funerals should always be dour affairs, clouded in incense with droned out rosaries and mumbled inane platitudes. But Thea's funeral was black and pink like a bag of liquorice allsorts. A celebration. The coffin was a simple pine construction with brass hinges in the shape of cockle shells. Placed on the top was a recent picture of Thea, a smile that lit up the world, encased in a silver frame. On the offertory table on the altar, the priest, Fr Gibney, informed the congregation of the totems that Thea loved; a tatty, much loved, and much washed Garfield toy, her sunglasses, a signed Ireland rugby shirt (she had told Crowe that every summer she played tag rugby) her favourite hoodie, and her pink apron from the Boogie-Woogie Café. Her phone though had not been found, and her iPad had been taken away by the investigating Gardai.

Crowe stood at the back of the church, hidden under the choir's balcony. Phones set on silent were still being scrolled, casting odd rectangles of light bobbing like mechanical fireflies. The organ above him groaned and the choir seemed choked. Notes drifted astray into the eaves. Crowe folded his arms and closed his eyes. His mind began to hop, he thought about and ruled out the three pups that day in the Café. They were yahoos, but not murderers. *If* this was a murder. He opened his eyes and scanned the silent congregation; Derry had dialled down the showbiz, but still managed to nod and glad hand his way to the front. His hair seemed to have gone a shade darker and his pink tie could probably be seen from space.

Then Crowe spied the librarian. She was picking her way along the far side of the church, looking for a gap in the pews. She looked like she was concentrating on the act of just moving forward. Her sunglasses were welded to her nose. Figure-of-eighting, followed by an unsteady genuflection, the sunglasses found him, and she weaved her way up beside him. He inched sideways and she wedged herself in.

She smelled of mouthwash and another fainter undertow as she whispered,

"Thanks,"

The unseasonably warm day and press of warm bodies added a new oppression to the atmosphere. She was sweating. He could smell it.

"Clodagh," she said.

"Crowe,"

"Apt," she muttered.

Fr Gibney celebrated the mass, people stood, kneeled, and sat. Rites and chanted replies were punctuated by snuffled sobs from the front pews.

"Isn't it awful?," said Clodagh, just a pitch too loud.

A couple of faces turned from the seats to stare at them.

Crowe pressed his back deeper into the wall,

"Terrible," he said.

Gibney, a frail stick of a man removed his glasses and adjusted the microphone while leaning in to deliver the final reel of his homily,

"You may, or may not have heard of Morris West, he's one of my favourite authors. A passage of his comes to mind when I think of Thea, Andrew and Grace here today" he cleared his throat,

"*'I know what you are thinking – you need a sign, what better one could I give than to make this little one whole and new? I could do it, but I will not, I am the lord and not a conjuror. She will never offend me as all of you have done, she will never pervert or destroy the work of my father's hand. She is necessary to you to evoke kindness that will keep you human'* – that's what Thea did for this parish, this town, she evoked kindness. Young Thea Louise Farrell kept us all human. Don't worry, be happy."

The old and bent priest let the sentence hang.

A cathartic yell and a lengthy round of applause filled the old stone church. Then the organ wheezed to life and somehow Thea was everywhere in the church. Crowe didn't believe in ghosts, though destroyed existences spoke to him sometimes in dreams. But if they did exist, right here, right now, Thea was amid her kith and kin.

From the front pew, came a guttural shriek. A sound that could have been howled at the dawn of mankind, the cry of a grieving mother. Grace tore out into the aisle and wrapped her arms around the coffin. It teetered on its trellis. Her wails were heart rending. Her face, contorted grief. The congregation stood stock still as if frozen. In his youth, Crowe had seen a foal struck and killed on the road by a truck. The sounds its mother made as she tossed and bucked were the same. Eventually, some relatives stirred and placed their arms around Grace, while the husband hovered around the edge.

She shrugged them off,

"Fuck you. Fuck off, Andrew - Fuck you all!" she screamed.

Clodagh Robertson bent forward and vomited up a small stream of Pernod. The acidic blast of aniseed filled the space between her and Crowe. It sloshed messily on their shoes and tiled floor.

"Better get some air," said Crowe.

He guided Clodagh out gently by the elbow into the sunlight, inwardly furious. He wanted to see Andrew Farrell escort his dead daughter's coffin up the aisle and into the hearse. To see Daddy's face up close. Because Mammy had told him to fuck-off in front of six-hundred people.

"Do you smoke?" asked Crowe.

"I'd kill for one now," replied Clodagh,

As Crowe lit her up, Clodagh cupped his hands in hers as she bent into the smoke. Their touch, skin-to-skin sent his nerve ends into an unexpected surge.

They stood like two sullen teenagers hauled to the church to make the pledge after an all-night cider party. The smoke eddied around them like sulphur on the breeze.

"Going to the grave?" he asked.

"I don't know the family that well. Have you a first name?"

Crowe said nothing,

"Man of few words,"

Crowe shrugged.

"I could always invent one for you," she said.

"P," he started, then paused on a drag, "tell me – are you living here long?"

"Six months. I was born here, got married, that didn't work out so well. Moved back to care for my mother and became a librarian. I see you most mornings,"

"I didn't see…"

"I kayak every morning. I saw you searching."

"I never noticed," said Crowe.

She pulled deeply on the cigarette,

"No-one ever does,"

Then she tilted her head. The sunglasses seemed to peer deeper into him. Crowe could see his reflection in the lenses,

"You're the guard who was all over the news? The one who attacked that poor man in the tracksuit."

"It was a disagreement," he said putting an end to that conversation, "Touching that," he continued.

"What?" said Clodagh.

"The things that defined Thea. Her personal possessions on the altar."

"Missed that bit trying to find a seat. Sad. Were her medals there?"

Crowe couldn't be sure what she had said. Slurring from the booze and inhaling the smoke had made it sound like Metal. Menthol. Meddle. Meth?

"Sorry, repeat that?"

Clodagh Robertson flicked the half-finished butt. It arced over the stone path to the neatly tended grounds in a final blaze of glory.

She reached into her shoulder bag and took out a stick of chewing gum. She popped it in her mouth,

"Her medals, Thea was a special Olympian. She was a water baby," said Clodagh.

"It was never mentioned," started Crowe.

"Silver – two of them. Swimming." A grating smugness had crept into her.

"No. Just a Garfield, a few gewgaws," said Crowe.

"Gewgaws?"

A Kind of Drowning

The hangover had shifted her polarity; a sneer had crept into the smug. It drifted on the blast of peppermint as it slid across her face.

Crowe's phone beeped. The number carried the Dublin prefix.

"Gotta go," he said.

"Thanks for the ciggy…?" said Clodagh.

"John,"

"I thought your name began with 'P'?" she said.

"*P* is for Podge,"

"That's a real hick name,"

"I'm a real hick at heart,"

"I'll stick with John,"

But Crowe had already turned on his heel. He thumbed the dial on the mobile retuning Olivia Cutts' text message.

If he had looked back, he would have seen Clodagh Robertson slowly engulfed by a tide of pink and black.

14

It was doubtful that Mulligans Bar on the main street of Roscarrig had seen anything like Dr. Olivia Cutts in its lifetime. She breezed in through the frosted double doors like it was the Cannes Film Festival.

"Jesus, Pink hair Crowe. Is it panto season already? The state of you," she said, "what is so urgent that you need me to trek out here?"

"I was at Thea Farrell's funeral yesterday. Speaking of which…?"

"I'm doing, well, thank you very much," she replied.

Cutts swung her satchel onto the table, sliding the condiments basket to the table's edge.

Her hair hung in lingering jet-black coils as she opened out the folder. Her perfect mouth set to concentration. Her nails flicking through the A4 sheets were gothic black. She pulled out a folded photocopy and shrugged off her expensive lime green jacket, peppered with droplets of rain. Smart pleated slacks and stylish blouse beneath accentuated her form. Patent black leather Doc Martens shone like pools of Indian ink.

"This is against regulations, Podge," she said.

"I'm well aware of that, Liv."

"If anyone at HQ thinks I'm meeting you, I'll be on the Commissioner's carpet right after HR are finished with me, P. Seriously."

Five fishermen clumped in through the door, casting curious looks at the marvellous creature that had beamed down from another world. Cutts ignored their admiring glances in a manner that suggested this was a daily chore.

She leaned in, her small dark eyes burrowed deep out of perfectly arched eyebrows,

"Thea Farrell: Our mystery girl, death by misadventure. Simple as."

"Can I see your findings?"

"No,"

Crowe looked at Cutts. He detected pity as well as annoyance. He decided not to push his luck.

"Are you driving?" he asked.

"Since yesterday, feels like. This really is the back of beyond – two hours in the fucking traffic this morning. I'll have a coffee – Cappuccino."

"Anything to eat?"

"Start with the coffee. If its instant, I'll pass, thanks."

A bored looking barman stared out into the middle distance; a face that managed to heap disappointment onto total disinterest in his existence. He half-heartedly swirled a cloth around the coasters along the bar. A man out of time and location; he looked like he should be in LA making lattes for the Hollywood set.

"A Cappuccino, please. Large and I'll have an Americano, no milk with a Jemmy on the side," said Crowe.

"Were you at Thea Farrell's funeral?" asked the Barman. His tattoos started at the strong knuckles and surged up his well-toned arms. His beard looked like it had been painted on. Crowe wondered why a generation was etching itself in expensive ink. He prayed that Cathal wouldn't get one.

"What gave it away?" asked Crowe.

"Your hair, pal," replied the barman.

Crowe looked at his own gnarled hands. He remembered the unexpected pulse of heat from Clodagh Robertson's touch. Could flesh convey intent? Locard's Principal – every contact leaves a trace. Clodagh's hand had done that; offering dangerous possibilities. He glanced down at his vomit splashed running shoe.

"Yep, sad," he said.

"The father was a great footballer in his day, local hero, minor county medals," said the barman nodding towards the team photos lining the far wall.

To Crowe's surprise, the bar had a glittering coffee machine that looked capable of barista warp nine.

"He buried his daughter today," said Crowe, "I'm sure he'd swap them all just to have her back,"

He thought of the maudlin cortege meandering through the narrow town, out the narrow road to the small wind blasted graveyard overlooking the Irish Sea. Thea's bed for eternity.

"Dublin panel is intense, man. *Intense* – even to get called up to the minors is a miracle – he could have gone all the way, Croker final. AFL down under – Sydney Swans were ready to sign him, and then…"

Old instincts die hard and Crowe's began to gnaw at him. In his previous life he'd start mining into this, the questions were gathering on the tip of his tongue; but Cutts was on a clock and he needed her now. Maybe another time. He held up a hand.

"He lost a child – Thea. Her name is Thea. I think that's more important. I'm not paying you to chat, I'm paying you to pour a drink."

The fishermen bunched into a corner and snapped out pocketed tabloids, working their way from the sports pages to the front. Betting slips appeared. Mobile phones offered odds. The coffee machine hissed and spat out Crowe's orders. A glass of whiskey accompanied by a small jug of water was handed to Crowe. He nudged the water to one side. At least Mr Ink hadn't put ice in the shot. The men studied Crowe from head to foot, bemused at his hair then returned to their on-line punts, smelling cop off him, and inching away fractionally.

Crowe's eyes drifted along the bar. An entire wall was filled with generations of Roscarrig's GAA teams. Each picture had a year engraved into a brass plate. He walked over for a closer look. Line after line of passion, honour, and pride; captured in black and white up to present day colour. And there, Andrew Farrell stared out of the glass. He was front row, knuckles clenched. He looked to Crowe like a man whose vision was forever elsewhere. A never smiling existence, dreaming of the next horizon. You got men like that sometimes in all walks of life; throw a stone in a Garda station locker room and you'd hit a man like that. Probably two.

Crowe's eyes fell onto Liv who was motioning to look behind him. Her flawless features mouthed *For Fuck's Sake.*!

"Coffee's going cold, bud," said the barman.

Crowe walked back and threw some cash onto the bar, and brought the drinks over, tucking the food menu under an armpit.

"How are you doing anyway, Podge?" she asked.

"Middling to fair,"

"Alison, Cathal?"

"Haven't heard from either," mulled Crowe.

"Not surprised."

"Cheers for that. You? Still separated?"

"Decree Absolute last year. Changed my name back – a pain in the hole to be honest."

Now ex-husband, Shay. Seamus Ahern, top-gun barrister, Twitter handle, '@ShayDubMaverickSC' had finally upped stakes and walked out. Olivia was off-the-chart smart and maybe he couldn't handle it. Crowe had seen her throw a punch or two over the years. Some men just couldn't deal with superior intelligence and firepower.

"Now, our poor little water baby," began Cutts. She pulled a loose strand of hair and wound it around her ear. Piercings peppered it and a long slender earring swayed as she spoke,

"Facial recognition was pretty poor, a fair bit of damage as a result of a long submersion. First Guard on the scene, Boyle, cordoned off as per SOP. Logged time and date. Took statements from the fishermen who brought her up. She was pronounced at the scene and life extinct confirmed by the paramedics – it took them nearly two hours to get here incidentally from call-out to arrival."

"Life on a peninsula. There's a local doctor, O'Rourke" said Crowe

"Couldn't be found, but everything seems to have been by the book as far as I can see."

Crowe thought about Thea lying on the quayside, on display to all, landed like an early morning catch. Shiny and bloated.

"Did you perform the post-mortem?"

Cutts took a sip from her coffee, some froth gathered at her upper lip, she licked it away. Crowe poured the whiskey into his Americano.

"Yep. I surmised she was in the water for over seventy-two hours, quite a bit of saline degradation from the immersion on her extremities. Her eyes were gone, probably seagulls, common for this

A Kind of Drowning

kind of death. Finger scrapings and nail clippings – nil result. No trace evidence to indicate a struggle. No alcohol or drugs in her system. DNA; Buccal, muscle, blood – nil result. Dental was a bit messed up, but if she fell near rocks, the tide would have bashed her head about. Either that or the side of the boat that found her. Poor lamb."

"Rape kit?" asked Crowe

"Negative result. No signs of any sexual activity."

"Lungs?"

"She drowned, P, though there were some plant seeds present which means she inhaled some flora before death. Rock samphire. When the water entered her lungs, her body vomited up her stomach contents, I found a few of these seeds around her nasal cavity, under her tongue and at the back of her throat. Thea possibly took a wrong step, slipped, banged her head, fell into the sea. It all points in the direction of an accident. The final report will be death by misadventure."

"These seeds, this samphire, is it common to this area?" asked Crowe.

"Not sure, Podge,"

Crowe mulled on this.

"Breakages?" he asked.

"Upper arms. And her lower legs. Though, and this would raise a minor concern; lack of bruising around two of the leg fractures,"

"Meaning?"

"It's possible *slightly possible* she fell from a height."

Where was she and what had she been doing? Thought Crowe. Height? It was only beaches and dunes around here?

A Kind of Drowning

Cutts took out a silver pen from her satchel. Crowe had bought it for her years ago as a birthday gift. A silver Cross pen. She folded over the photocopy and made a mark. Her expression became focussed.

"No other injuries, post, peri or antemortem to suggest an attack or struggle in any way. Clothes had no discernible DNA transfer, no damage – she was missing a NIKE running shoe - left foot. She'd had a vegetable curry with boiled rice, mostly digested at time of death," she continued. Then she looked up. She knew Crowe. Before becoming the laughing stock of the force, he was rarely, if ever, wrong on a hunch.

"Where are you going with this, Podge?"

"I'm ordering a ham and cheese toastie – you?" said Crowe.

"Do they have gluten-free?"

"I've said it before, that's all in your head."

"Fuck off you fat bastard – see if they have gluten free sandwiches?"

"Unicorn fries on the side?" he grinned

"Asshole."

"Pixie-dust to sprinkle on?"

Crowe waved the creased menu toward the barman.

"Come over and order it, I'm not a waiter, bud." He said.

"Keep working that magic, Podge," said Cutts.

Crowe yelled, "Two ham and cheese toasties, extra mustard on mine, gluten free for the lady and two more coffees and another jemmy, por favor."

The barman ambled off on his quest for something other than a sliced batch loaf.

"Thea Farrell was a swimmer – special Olympian. Two silver medals in the special Olympics. Liv. Not just a paddler or a splasher – a medal winner," said Crowe.

He flashed up his Google search on his phone – Special Olympics Ireland. There was a picture of a much younger Thea, about fourteen years old. Grinning happily and holding two medals up.

"Medal winner," repeated Crowe.

Cutts' expression flashed from *so what?* to something else.

She pulled out her iPhone,

"Her BMR was good, certainly not overweight. No underlying health issues. Fuck. Jesus. No signal here? Is there even any Wi-Fi in this place?"

"It's a bit Land-that-Time-Forgot out here," said Crowe.

"We have spelt – will that do?" shouted over the barman.

"One spelt and one normal toastie. Fries with both, merci beaucoup," shouted Crowe.

He ignored Cutts' middle finger.

"I'm not ruling out an accident, Liv – look at Ayrton Senna. But something about this doesn't pass the smell test."

"Jaysus, Crowe – quoting Quigley – what's he up to these days?"

"Moving into property lettings, apparently," replied Crowe.

"Evictions are up according to the papers these days, no better man. Is he still singing?" said Cutts.

"Everyone keeps asking me that, I'm his tenant, not his roadie,"

"Does one mean 'Old Man River'. Gives Paul Robeson a run for his money."

"Haven't seen or heard from him, Liv, if I do, I'll send him your regards," he lied. Upper Cutts as she was known, had once threatened Quigley with a kicking he'd never forget.

"International Man of Mystery? Nah, you're alright, he's far too familiar with his hands."

Cutts elegantly moved her iPhone around the air, searching for an elusive signal. Her other hand tapped the silver pen on the table in a paradiddle.

"Thea's medals weren't on display – not a mention," said Crowe.

"Why would the family *not* mention it?" asked Cutts.

Crowe looked over at the picture where the unsmiling Andrew Farrell glowered out,

"No idea, Liv,"

The food arrived and Crowe emptied a sachet of vinegar over thick-cut fries,

"All the basic food groups covered, I see," said Cutts.

"I'm a growing lad,"

"Mostly outward, Crowe. It's never too late for exercise,"

"I'm comfortable with who I am."

"I'll remember that if you ever wind up on my slab," replied Cutts.

A Kind of Drowning

Crowe devoured the sandwich almost whole. A thick web of molten cheese caught in his stubble. With his uneven pink hair, he seemed more of a train wreck than ever thought Cutts.

But she remembered that he had once saved her career and taken a fall for her.

"When was your last medical?" she asked.

"Disciplinary – two months ago. Fit as a fiddle,"

"The irony," she replied.

Crowe polished off the second part of the sandwich and moving most of it to the side of his jowl asked,

"I think it's more than a drowning,"

Cutts shuddered,

"Fuck, Crowe, close your mouth - that was disgusting. On paper, it's an accident. Teenagers drown. Case closed."

"Well, if she fell, where did she fall from?" he asked.

Cutts unrolled the knife from the napkin in slow winds. Her wrists, like her fingers were long and fine boned. Scalpels were merely extensions, thought Crowe.

"Can't help you there, Podge. Like I said an open and shut case. You'll need more than a hunch, knowing something and proving it are two completely different things."

"Yeah, but judging by your expression, I've kicked the case's lock a bit."

She sliced the sandwich up and chewed delicately. Her middle-distance gaze freeze-framed her beauty. A woman who inspired poetry.

A Kind of Drowning

"On balance, Podge, I'd let this one go. This isn't inner city, no fucked-up shit, nothing I saw indicated anything nasty took place. We're in the middle of nowhere. Our water baby died in the middle of nowhere. If she fell, she could have been stunned, got into difficulty. End-of."

But a shadow flitted across her eyes as she spoke.

"In a sleepy little town called Roscarrig," said Crowe.

"Accidents happen, Podge,"

Cutts reached into her purse,

"Is there a petrol station nearby?" she asked.

She dabbed her mouth with a napkin. She slid the folder toward him.

"Turn left, follow the coast road. One on the right," said Crowe.

"Back in a minute, don't leave any stains or ketchup fingerprints, yeah? This is the last favour, P, and don't look at me that way. We are quits after this."

She strode out of the bar like a green cloaked Valkyrie and Crowe thumbed his way carefully through her report.

He mashed the last of the sandwich into his mouth.

"Got a pen?" he shouted to the barman

A biro was chucked towards him.

Taking a napkin from the table beside him, he made a few notes,

He was going to need a white board, blue tack, string, and paper. A meaty obsession beckoned; one that would give him an anchor to reality. He waited for Cutts. She was always worth the wait.

15

"Harris, you busy?" asked Crowe.

There was a long pause on the other end of the line, "Who is this?" answered Harris.

"Crowe," he crunched the mobile up to his ear with his shoulder as he unpacked a few groceries.

"For fuck's sake, where the hell are you? Leaving me hanging like a gimp at the moment," Union Rep Harris' nasal drone lost some of its carefully measured cadences,

"Off-grid and chilling by the sea, taking the waters as they say, which brings me to my question," said Crowe.

There was a measured silence now.

"Desmond Cosgrave, aka, Teflon D, is rumoured to have moved into a seaside town. Are you taking this down?"

"Nope," replied Harris evenly,

"Great. Heard there was an attempt on his life in Dublin, and he's fled to the sticks. I'm wondering if his operations have moved with him too?"

"In case you've forgotten, Podge, you are suspended? What's going on? Where the fuck are you? O'Suilleabháin's been asking if anyone has heard from you lately."

"Roscarrig,"

"Never heard of it,"

"Exactly. One horse town with a big island on its doorstep. And Teflon D just put down stakes."

There was the sound of the receiver being muted and Harris' voice pitched low, indistinct.

"I'm a union rep, Crowe, not the bloody NBCI," he paused, "Leave it with me,"

But Crowe could hear an inflection, an interest. He could picture Harris' eyes beginning to flicker under the generally inert eyelids,

"Give that to me again?", a scratching of a pencil came down the line,

"Roscarrig. Big Island nearby: Inishcarrig – see if anything pops up?" said Crowe.

"I'll get back to you. Oh, and Crowe?"

"Yep?"

"You ok? Minding yourself?"

"Fair to middling – how quickly can you get back to me?"

"I'll just stop all my actual fucking work and do your bidding?"

"That's the spirit, Harris," replied Crowe.

"You know, Crowe, you could just try Googling all of this?"

"You know me, Harris, I'm a digital luddite,"

"A lazy bastard more like,"

Harris hung up.

He was back thirty minutes later, as Crowe was heating up baked beans in the microwave. Toast was slowly blackening in the unpredictable toaster.

"Ok, Crowe, I did a little digging around PULSE and made a phone call. This is strictly off the record. Now, Teflon D, how long have you got with this character? Word is that he's ear-marked for assassination; some local feud, and he's lying low…"

"…In Roscarrig," said Crowe, "That's a confirmation, so. What else?"

Harris cleared his throat, "His move hasn't disrupted his business, still plenty of drugs coming in and making their way onto the street. But – pay a-fucking-ttention, Podge, there's a lot of radio silence around his name, which would suggest to me, INTERPOL are working with our lads in the GNDU and the DPP. His missues fucked off to Spain last year and we suspect she's the initial point of contact and general logistics for the drug shipments. This is all pointing to a bust. You know how long these things take to put together, so stay the fuck away from this guy."

"So I've been told. Then our boy, Teflon probably has a boat and a point of landing?" asked Crowe.

He coloured in a doodle of a boat as he listened to Harris shuffling papers.

"Yup," replied Harris, "Now this gets interesting. Your big island, Inishcarrig, it's for sale by private treaty. Ephraim Hunt – the legend of the confiscated portfolios, bids, tenders, and plans by NAMA. That hasn't stopped this joker putting a bid in on this island,"

Crowe's mind began to whirr,

"Major drug lord and a property developer in the same neck of the woods? Bet Teflon wouldn't like Hunt pissing all over his patch. Would you have a recent photo of Teflon?"

"I can't do that, Crowe, you know the rules. Though, I can suggest you go to the on-line Daily Star. Are you on your phone? Its dated three weeks ago. His two sprogs, Fionn and Setanta signed a major record deal. K-Pop shite. Our boy Teflon's in the background. Far right in the photo. Have you found it?"

Crowe double-tapped the image to increase the magnification. No doubt about it.

"Gotta go, Harris, have to see a man about a dog. Thanks for your help,"

Crowe hung up before Harris could reply.

***

The Staffordshire bull terrier was ploughing along the sand with compact meaty strides. Crowe could hear it panting as it strained against its harness. The twilight gave its wet coat an added sheen, no doubt contented at being hurled on a daily basis into the surf at the lifeboat station. The man with the baseball cap pulled low matched the photo. Crowe was staring at Teflon D.

"Got a light, bud?" asked Crowe,

"Don't smoke, pal. Sorry," replied Teflon.

The Staffy squatted and defecated gloriously. Once it had finished, Teflon banked the sand up in careful nudges over the turds with his expensive looking runners. Five rings of fat supported Teflon's skull. From what Crowe could see, the fat merged with the shoulders somewhere below the ears. One threaded eyebrow had three thin razored lines cut in. The eyes were blue, unblinking, reptilian. Teflon D was a mass of Hi Viz waterproof jacket with the collar turned up and black ADIDAS.

"The tide will wash it away," he replied, judging Crowe's expression. The beach was deserted anyway. Crowe jammed the cigarette in under his cap.

A Kind of Drowning

"That's some island," he said, nodding to Inishcarrig. The light was fading fast, turning the greens and ambers to a lifeless looking dun. The sea between churned darkly.

"Roman coins were found there," said Teflon.

The dog was sitting on its hip on the sand. The tail thumped in thick swings,

"Quadrans with the face of Hadrian, two earthen jars found buried intact were full of them. They were excavated on the far side of the island," said Teflon. He gave the leash a gentle whip, but the staffy was staying put. It jerked its head back and forth between Crowe and Teflon displaying jowly rows of fangs, wheezing like a bellows between intermittent growls.

"History buff?" asked Crowe.

Teflon cracked a smile,

"Amateur, bud. An amateur. Seems there was trade between here and Roman Britain. Then came the Vikings. Just past the tower there they found more coins, Viking silver, dated 995 to 998, CE."

"CE?" asked Crowe.

"*'Common Era'*, they're phasing out Anno Domini, bud. No more Jesus, it upsets the other faiths,"

"Not a bad idea," said Crowe, "Are there still archaeological digs going on the island?" he continued.

"No, Not since the financial crash. Everything stopped, the archaeologists all packed up and left."

"Romans, Vikings, Napoleon, any old smuggler's caves? Looks like the perfect location for a bit of piracy and running a bit of contraband. You should do a YouTube talk, post it up," said Crowe.

"Not my scene, sport. Leave all that social media malarkey to the next generation. Nice talking to you."

Teflon made a clicking sound and the dog began to stir. Without warning it made a lunge towards Crowe, jaws snapping. Crowe stood his ground,

"Not very friendly is he?" he said.

Teflon wrangled the animal back with a grin,

"Hates coppers, but I reckon he's homesick or hungry,"

"You're not local then?" asked Crowe.

"Just passing through," replied Teflon.

Crowe could sense that Teflon was taking him in. The eyes beneath the cap carefully scanned the worn shoes, the shapeless pants and tattered fleece jacket. He might have looked like a vagrant on a day out, but the dog wasn't fooled.

"Same here," said Crowe.

"Stay off the coffin nails," said Teflon, "My Da was an eighty a day man. Killed him in his fifties. Cancer."

"I'll bear that in mind," said Crowe.

Teflon had kept one hand out of sight, buried into the jacket's pocket. Crowe wondered if it was the hand with the missing thumb. He debated following Teflon, weighed it up in his mind, but as they were the only souls on the beach it would look obvious. In the gathering evening light, Crowe waited until Teflon had left the beach.

He sparked up his cigarette.

Teflon was right, the tide had flowed in, each wave covering the dog shit.

A Kind of Drowning

The sea water lapped greedily around Crowe's heels as he smoked and watched the receding figure. It wasn't lost on him that if it hadn't been for them, Crowe would have ended up tagged in the morgue as a suicide.

Teflon and his dog disappeared into shadows, mottled in pulses of sea spray. In the gathering night, the island felt like a magnet drawing everyone and everything toward it. It both anchored and repelled the town, like some silent, festering cancerous cell.

He finished his smoke and crushed the butt into the soaking sand and decided that tomorrow, he'd stop by and make a sympathy call.

16

Crowe couldn't count how many times he had made the walk up a pathway to someone's home to deliver the worst possible news. His gut twisted instinctively as he opened the old fashioned wrought iron gate to Thea's home. More and more of his wrecked police nerve-endings were starting to reconnect and spark. The house was a renovated two-storey with a red brick façade. Everything apart from the gate looked spruce, modern, and well maintained. The windows shone in front of white New England shutters slanted closed, stifling any available sunlight. The driveway had an engine oil stain, framed by faded tyre tracks that reminded Crowe of a birthmark. This led via a shady passage to a gate into the back garden. A wall-mounted basketball hoop stood forlorn and limp on the corner of the house, the netting swaying in the sea breeze.

It was unseasonably warm. The sun burned through the sky and made Crowe sweat beneath his fleece as he rang the doorbell. Somehow it seemed the most silent house on the planet. The shuttered interiors inhabited by ghosts.

He gave the bell two more presses.

He heard the sound of a key turning and Grace Farrell stood staring at him. Her clothing was as uncoordinated and misshapen as his,

"I've come to pay my respects, Mrs Farrell," said Crowe, "my deepest condolences on your loss,"

Grace's skin was sere in the harsh sunlight. She had clearly abandoned make up. Her hair hung limp and unwashed. She was a woman barely forty now passing for seventy.

"Thank you," she murmured, then gave a sudden shake, "I'm sorry, I don't recognise you?"

"My name is John, I worked in the café with her, with Thea,"

Grace's gaze suddenly bored into Crowe, starting with his unkempt pink hair, and working down taking in every inch of him. She showed a flicker of pity at the state of his shoes.

"Mr. Grumpy?"

"Yes. That was Thea's name for me. She was an amazing, wonderful soul,"

"She talked about you a lot. Come in. I have a pot of tea on."

"I won't take too much of your time," said Crowe.

"I've all the time in the world," she said.

The hall was a shrine to Andrew Farrell, the footballer. Every inch of wall space was covered with him and older photographs of a man who must have been his father. Both sinewy warriors in shorts and football jerseys. A framed newspaper article showed the father and son holding a trophy and grinning broadly. As Crowe walked along the hall he glanced at more pictures of numerous golf outings, groups of men all red-eyed and shiny behind the glass.

There were no pictures of Thea.

Laminate timber flooring, scuffed by countless boots and shoes led to a huge bright kitchen. A stack of unwashed pots and pans sat on the draining board. The kitchen smelled of old grease and fried bacon,

"Please, sit down," she said.

Crowe pulled a chair out; a smear of mud lay caked on the wooden seat. He eased himself down, avoiding as much of it as he could.

"How are you and your husband doing?" he asked, "Andrew isn't it?"

The ceramic teapot was shaking as Grace poured,

"Oh you know, day-by-day, one step-at-a-time, the usual…"

The tea spilled over the rim of the mug,

"That's perfect," said Crowe pulling the mug toward him, "Thank you, Mrs Farrell,"

"You can call me Grace, no need to be formal, John," she replied.

He sipped enough away to allow some milk. A small jug and a crystal sugar bowl were slid toward him across a table criss-crossed with dried-in cup rings. Grace had only one slipper on as she turned away from the table to put the pot on the counter. He piled in three heaped teaspoons and drank,

"Will you have one yourself?" he asked.

"I've had a bellyful of tea, thanks," she said.

Crowe had learned over the years that silence worked best. Whether it was the interview room or visiting a heart-broken family, saying nothing, and letting the person talk to a uniform was cathartic.

Except he wasn't in uniform.

He was almost at the end of the cup when Grace turned and looked back,

"I've never seen you before. Are you a blow-in?" she asked.

Crowe allowed a lop-sided smile,

"No. Just passing through. Derry Gallagher set me up for a few weeks. Which is why I'm here. I'd just like to say, before I move on, that Thea was a smashing kid,"

"She was. Yes. A gift," replied Grace.

Crowe nodded in agreement and downed the dregs. Leaves filled his tongue and gums. But it was worth it. Grace shuffled over with the pot. More tea spilled, but Grace's shaking had stopped,

"Yes, she was. Oh dear," she breathed. She got up again and shuffled toward a unit over the kitchen, she came back with a packet of cigarettes,

"Andrew never liked me smoking. I quit fifteen years ago, but now, I don't care," she said.

"Allow me," said Crowe.

He produced his lighter and his own pack. He offered her a light then lit up himself. Grace opened a side window bringing cool relief to the heat of the kitchen.

She continued, "Thank you. I did it for Thea, I wanted to be around as long as possible for her. We both knew that if she survived past thirty, it'd be a boon."

She stopped and jerked her head toward the back garden as if she had heard something, an echo or memory of Thea maybe? In profile, Grace Farrell was still a handsome woman.

"We, well, Andrew didn't want to go again. We were afraid we'd have another one. Andrew used to say he didn't want to inflict another one on the community,"

"Inflict? That's a bit harsh," said Crowe.

"I could see his point. Maybe if we'd had one that was... *healthy*, whole, complete – God forgive me, Thea would have had someone to watch over her, look out for her,"

"Not Thea's style," said Crowe.

Grace smiled thinly, "No. Not Thea's style. True. She was a fighter,"

Crowe followed Grace's gaze. At the back of the garden was a fence, and beyond the fence, the dunes to the sea.

"Tough as nails. Took no prisoners, that girl. How did Andrew take it? How is he coping?" asked Crowe.

Grace exhaled a long plume of smoke.

"Oh, he's busy, always busy, I'm married to a busy little bee – that's what Thea called him, *'our busy, busy bee.'* He's pinning his hopes on a new venture, he thinks there's going to be a big project for the town…"

Crowe remined silent. He swilled his tea as if divining the leaves swirling at the bottom.

"He works all the hours God gives him," said Grace, "he was always a good provider, and working for yourself is always 24/7, but I think he never wanted to be here with Thea and me. He used to run to his parents place, even when Thea was young. They put a brave face on it, but they never accepted Thea. The father couldn't bring himself to look at her. Sometimes he'd shout at her, and Andrew… Sorry," her voice caught on a rising swell of emotion but rode it on a breath, "…Andrew would never face him down, stand up for her…"

"I've taken up enough of your time," said Crowe. He started to rise, but Grace flapped an arm down.

"Sit. You're not like the rest of this town. We are a small fishing community. Tight knit, conservative and Catholic. I know when you leave none of this will matter. The problem here is we were all born in Roscarrig and we went from the primary school to the secondary, communion to confirmation, twenty firsts and weddings, then births, communion and confirmations – where are you from, John, may I ask?"

"Clonmel, the family eventually settled in Dublin," replied Crowe.

Grace nodded absently, "Everyone loved her, you see?, Thea. She was wilful, oh God, could be a wilful brat sometimes but pure, like?"

Crowe leaned a little forward, he wrapped his fingers around the cup. Grace took a long drag and continued,

"In some ways she was blessed. I wanted her to have a good life. I thought it would be a blessing that she'd never have children of her own. What sort of world would her children have with the climate crisis 'n all? In fifty years or so, Roscarrig will be under water and gone. Gone like Avalon. And this variant flu everyone's talking about? Another bloody virus. One after another? All we, no, all *I* wanted was for Thea to live out her life as full as possible... Her natural life. Not this. Fuck no, not this..."

Crowe put the empty cup down. He rose to leave, and Grace looked up,

"Thank you," she whispered.

"Lookit, tell you what, I'll give a hand over there," he nodded.

He motioned to the pile of pots and pans. The sink was full of unwashed delph too. Grace looked lost in her thoughts; the cigarette tip glowed with her breaths. Crowe ran the hot water tap and filled the sink with hot water. He located steel wool under the sink unit and scrubbed the pots thoroughly working the suds into the caked-in food. He worked in silence with his back to her as he wiped down the counter top. He could hear her let out long sighs. One sounded like a moan,

"It's not right. It doesn't *feel* right, you know? It was a stupid row with Andrew. If I hadn't lost my temper, she'd still be here. Poor Thea. We went to bed without looking in on her. We saw the light on under the door. Every single night we would look in and blow kisses, but we were exhausted…"

"Would it have been late?" asked Crowe.

"After midnight. Andrew was restless, he couldn't settle. Went back downstairs to watch Netflix or something. I thought he'd looked in on her… He told me he had, but he'd had a few cans, his little nightcaps. Do you think she suffered? They say it's a peaceful way to go,"

Crowe thought about all the bodies he had seen fished out of rivers, found on the shore, or removed from cars that had slipped accidentally off piers or deliberately driven into the water in a moment of despair. Nothing he ever saw behind the tape or in the morgue ever said 'peaceful'.

"I've no idea," he said.

The tears came now. In floods. Crowe looked at Grace Farrell as she folded over the table weeping. He stepped over and placed a hand on her shoulder gently,

"There we go, a little bit tidier," he said.

"Thanks, John," said Grace wiping her face with the heel of her hand.

Just as he reached the hall, he turned.

"Can I ask what the big project Andrew was going to be working on?" he asked.

"Andrew says the island is going to become a golf course or some sort of leisure resort – but you know small towns, rumour mills," said Grace.

"Cities are worse, believe me," said Crowe, "I'll let myself out,"

A Kind of Drowning

Crowe stepped into the sunlight and pulled the door shut. He stared up at the sun in the clear azure skies. It glinted off a passing aircraft making it look like a slow motion meteorite tearing across the sky.

What sort of world will Cathal's children have? He thought. Cathal was a constant dull ache in his heart. Crowe pondered if there was any hope of a reconciliation.

Crowe turned off the path and crossed the driveway to the side passage. He walked down it and came to a tall wooden gate. Like everything about the exterior, it was painted and well-maintained. Too high to peer over on his tiptoes he stepped back.

The over-revving of an engine made him turn. A white transit van pulled in and Andrew Farrell spotting Crowe, jumped out,

"What the hell are you doing?" he barked.

Crowe walked up, "Came to pay my respects,"

"What, by trying to get over my fence?"

Crowe could see Andrew Farrell had a zero to asshole setting that activated like a light switch.

"Chased a cat off your hardy perennials at the front, the dirty little bastard," said Crowe easing past Farrell. He proffered a hand, "My condolences again for your loss. Thea was a…"

"Just get the fuck off my property, yeah? Snooping around – are you the fucking press?"

"No. I used to work with her in The Boogie-Woogie,"

Andrew Farrell spun without a word and marched to his front door,

"If I catch you around here again, y'jackass. You'll wake up in A and E, yeah?" he yelled over his shoulder

A Kind of Drowning

Crowe slipped out and away down the street, memorising the van's number plate as he walked. Grace was right; it just didn't feel right.

A trick of the atmospherics made Inishcarrig appear closer, looming large and ominous in the sea. Beyond the island, gunmetal coloured thunderheads churned, and the first smatterings of rain peppered the concrete as he walked. As he passed The Boogie-Woogie, the brightly chalked sandwich board gave him an idea.

He mulled over it as he climbed the stairs to his garret.

17

The Boogie-Woogie's cooks Maciej and Pavel lived together along with four other Polish nationals at the edge of the town in a refurbished two storey house. Bunk beds were stacked in pairs into two cramped bedrooms. The toilet facilities were rudimentary at best and the rent affordable, but that was about to increase now that the summer season was almost here. In the confined space of the old house, they moved around. Both downed high protein shakes, sourdough bread and coffee for breakfast. Both shrugged on their clothes. Both moved in unison out of the house, down the road passing the field hands returning at dawn to their own tightly packed accommodation. Each group passing the other with the barest of nods.

Like two young hounds they walked to the Boogie-Woogie. Pavel ran up the shutters while Maciej input the alarm code and turned on the power. They hung up their jackets, reversed their peaked caps, donned their aprons, and stared in wonder at the gap left by the missing whiteboard where Mel drafted her master plans, rotas, and menus for the day. Screws and rawl plugs gone and a dusting of wall plaster on the floor.

"Maybe she won't notice?" murmured Pavel.

They both burst out laughing.

***

Crowe propped the whiteboard on the mantlepiece. It would be his case board from now on. The TV now consigned to the floor. Fishing the white board's pens out of his cargo pants he began to write.

On the table, now cleared of plates, whiskey glass and cutlery, he had an A4 pad, the napkin with Cutts' notes and a stack of bright red pens lifted from the betting shop in the town. It wasn't lost on him that all of these were technically stolen. Purloined. Requisitioned.

NTDK - **Not the drowning kind** was scrawled at the top of the board – this would be his code for Thea.

S = Suspects was the first heading of 3 rough columns.

The other two columns were **E = Evidence** and **C = Cutts**.

On the A4 he had jotted down a shopping list: a map of the area, rubber gloves, plastic bags, tie-wraps, and indelible pens. He wondered where he could get details of the tides and currents.

He lit a B&H and stared at the board. His next stop was going to be the library.

He checked his watch, only to find he still didn't have one.

He tried Cathal's number only to see NUMBER BLOCKED appear on the screen.

He googled the Library opening times and saw he had missed the opening hours. It was closed.

Clodagh Robertson had said she was a kayaker, maybe she could provide some answers.

Which reminded him. He brought the better pair of runners from the ledge; the smell of Pernod had disappeared after a scrubbing in the sink. The offering to the fox below, a full single had been opened and devoured without a gull in sight.

He had a plan and for the first time in months, a purpose. Today, he was a detective again. Two women had touched him – Robertson on the hand and Cutts' peck on the cheek – he began to feel alive again, like the world was returning to technicolour. It was going to be a good day.

18

The more Crowe thought about it, the more he became convinced that the answer had to be on the island. The dead always give you an answer, it was just a question of deciphering their clues. Crowe was sure now. He had walked the length of the coast, starting from the harbour and made his way along the stone and shale in a westerly direction. The runners were leaking, and his socks now, were just a mash of water and sand around his heel. Sometimes he slipped traversing the rocks. He would have to add Wellington Boots to the shopping list, he thought.

Inishcarrig loomed across the water. He stopped and took photos on his phone. From the pocket of his fleece, he pulled out a small jotter. The clutch of betting slips discarded now. Another step toward recovery; a notebook. With a wire spine. He sketched the island roughly with a pencil. How did Thea Farrell get out there? He wrote, THEA, THEA, THEA, THEA, THEA – it became a scrawl, the blunt nib smearing the page.

Fuck it, he thought.

From the bulky pockets of his cargo pants he tugged out his cigarettes and lighter and lit one. He inhaled the tobacco and held it down in his lungs. He exhaled slowly through his nostrils, watching the plumes snatched by the breeze and swirled into the sky.

A local girl, Thea probably knew every nook and cranny, the safe areas and the dangerous ones. Every kid in the world had a hiding place, a bolthole, somewhere to get away from the family. Somewhere they shouldn't be, which added to the thrill. Thea Farrell was an adventurer to the core.

Did she swim out to the island? The distance might be achievable for a trained swimmer. Thea had guts. It was possible. Coming over a gradual rise, he found a cove. It scalloped out into two craggy horns offering protection from the breeze. A thin pathway of flattened grass led to a smooth stretch of beach and Crowe revelled in the solitude. The clouds had broken, and a high vault of blue appeared over the sea. It was warm and sheltered enough for Crowe to sit and smoke. He shrugged off the fleece and spread it out like a blanket and eased himself down. High up on the tideline was a stack of lobster pots, weather-worn and covered in seaweed. He lit another smoke and closed his eyes.

How had she got out there? For a split second, he thought about the helicopter. Fell from a height. Bone damage and fractures would be worse though. Cutts couldn't give him a specific height and knowing Liv, her schedule would be too full for another meeting. She had spelled it out to him, he was a civilian now. With suspension from duty, he had no power of arrest, anything he did wouldn't hold up in any court case. His suspicions would have to be presented as that. Suspicions. The get-out-of-jail card of a serving member of a police force was gone.

He was Joe Public now.

He riffled the pages again. On paper in the cold light of day, it was an accident. Perhaps after she had been verbally attacked, he had become overly protective towards her? Taken it to heart? Why was he making assumptions in the face of facts; accidents happen? Scotoma, he shrugged; a blind spot, only seeing what his mind wanted to see.

You are a valuable human being...

Thea was valuable but the world had already moved on. Her voice was silenced. For that alone, she deserved this digging. Dredging for the truth. Andrew Farrell had diminished her value by leaving her medals off her coffin. Diminished an achievement greater than his. It was ugly. Controlling. If members of Special Olympics Ireland had been at the funeral, their presence had been muted. He thought about Grace's rage at Farrell. The screeched invective.

A Kind of Drowning

Every family has its secrets.

Plant seeds in Thea's lungs. Samphire, *sounds like sapphires,* he thought. Had she been pushed face first onto the ground? Had she been forced *into* the ground? The sea damage to her face would've masked any superficial bruising. The gulls taking out her eyes too would have added more damage. No DNA under her fingernails.

Cutts had also said Thea was missing a running shoe. A white NIKE. If little else, it gave Crowe a reason to walk along the beach again. He checked his watch to tell the time, only he didn't have a watch.

He needed to get onto the island.

Crowe rose, dusted himself down and shook out the fleece. He folded away the jotter and checked the cigarettes – he was down to two. He lit one and put the other behind his ear, pushing his cap down to hold it secure. Ambling up the jagged horn of rock and grass, he bent down and pulled up a few plants that had begun to bloom. He turned them over in his hands, holding them up; what *exactly* was he looking for? He tried Googling 'Samphire', but the signal was non-existent. He placed the few plants in the cigarette box and hoisted himself back towards the harbour.

At the top of the dune, he looked down into the sea, the concertinaed rocks glowed in the sunlight's refraction. Deep green and blue blended into the darkness of the deep channel. Buoys bobbed lazily on the currents and the sea was smooth like glass. He panned his view slowly. Roscarrig; the sprawl of housing, old fisherman crofts and newly built starter homes with washing lines fluttering bright pennants of clothing. His eyes followed the dune lines to the rows of back gardens, greenhouses, and public parking areas. In one of the gardens the faint barks of a dog drifted across the sand.

Somebody must have seen her. Thea by her very nature would draw attention, she was noticeable.

A Kind of Drowning

A young woman walking alone at night.

Crowe slid down the far side of the rise, stumbling at the bottom and giving his ankle a hearty twist. Cursing and swearing, he limped along the shore on the look-out for a solitary shoe.

What else were Sundays for?

19

It was a suicide Monday when Clodagh spotted Crowe loitering at the library entrance. A morning that had felt like limbo as she left her house. As she free-wheeled toward the library, she had a momentary flashback of throwing up on his shoes. The same ones he was wearing today.

She felt exhausted. Her mother, Mary, had left her bed at two in the morning to start cleaning down the kitchen and had knocked over the mop and bucket, spilling suds, and detergent over the floor. Mother, Old Woman, Burden, turning on every light in the house as she went about her business. She didn't have a name now; she was an object, a diminished outline - a ghost. By the time she had settled *Mother* down, returning *The Old Woman* to bed and cleaned up, *The Burden* had left Clodagh sitting at the kitchen table watching the hands of the clock crawl around to morning. She would be forty-one next month and the sands were accelerating through the hour glass with nothing at the end to show for it. Breakfast had been a double vodka followed by another. Neat. Then a sugar-laden instant coffee. In the shower, Clodagh had pendulumed the water from freezing to scalding and back. Her skin bristled from the harsh towels. Perfect for her purgatory.

She left a small bowl of cereal and milk on the table. She wrote a note to the *oldwomanburden* upstairs, sleeping ever longer into the day, that she wouldn't be home to prepare lunch. There was a sandwich in the fridge and some scones in the bread bin.

Clodagh was too drained mentally and emotionally to kayak today. The vessel exorcised her shame and loathing in precise strokes, forcing her pace each morning against the current and the tides.

Crowe must have really gone to town on the dye as his hair was still a wild, matted bubble-gum colour. It poked out from under the cap in jarring sparks. Under the battered fleece, which looked suspiciously like the one she had seen hanging on a rail in the charity shop a few days earlier was a book. He was cradling it like a child.

She had thought of him amid her early morning chaos, that slow appearance in the mind of someone you sensed was like you. A kindred. Someone who crept into your mind unannounced that you knew was thinking of you. He stood less awkwardly, as if the conversation between them was already half-way through. He dropped his cigarette into a disposable coffee cup, and she watched him scan around for a bin.

"Library will open in fifteen minutes," she said.

"I'll wait," he replied.

She locked the bike with the heavy chain she carried in her handle bars basket. In her reflective yellow back pack was a carton of microwaveable soup and her bottle of water.

"There's a bin on Main Street," she said, eyeing the disposable cup Crowe was about to drop on the ground, "those cups aren't recyclable,"

Crowe seemed uncertain; a flash of confusion slid across his face.

"I'll wait," he said.

"Then wait," replied Clodagh.

Fifteen minutes later, he was on the opposite side of her desk. He handed her the book.

"You can scan it…" she started.

"You said you saw me every day on the beach? During the search?" said Crowe.

The book in his outstretched hand waivered slightly. He had big hands. In his lifetime, Crowe, the battered barn door, had performed heavy labour.

"I said that?" she said

"You did,"

"I can't remember, yes, possibly," she said as she took the book.

The plastic cover had a fresh cup ring right in the middle of it. It hadn't been there when he had taken it out.

"Would you have a map of the area?" he asked.

"Map?" she thought about it, "yes, there should be one in the town records on the second floor, far right-hand side, after the biography section."

"Not in a book. A fold-out? Is that one?"

She hadn't noticed it before, but Crowe had started living up to his name – the slight tilt of the head as his eyes with their anthracite glint scanned and filed everything. He had already spied the large ordinance map of the town and island mounted on the wall behind her desk. His mastiff mouth was set to a grin.

"You can't have that Crowe."

"Can I borrow it?"

"No. Don't force me to ask you to leave."

"It's a library – I see DVDs, CDs, Magazines to borrow…?"

"The answer is still no,"

Her 'No' sounded like biting down on tinfoil. It sliced across the desk.

"Thanks. One other thing," said Crowe

"Yes?"

"I need to get out there. To the island."

"It's private property,"

"It's for sale."

"Win the lottery?"

"Derry has connections, apparently, I'd like to visit,"

"I'm sure one of the fishermen would charter a boat out for the day. Derry, bless him, thinks he has his finger on the pulse, but the world just side-steps him,"

"I'd like to charter you," said Crowe

"In my kayak?"

"Boat, whatever. You know the currents, the tides, the best time to go."

"You could just Google all those details you know."

"I tried, but the signal is poor – next stop is here. Do you have anything bigger...?"

"Crowe, there is no way I could take a man of your size out to that island and back on my own – have you ever been in a kayak before?"

"No, but it doesn't look hard... I've... good upper-body strength."

Clodagh stared at him.

"I'm not talking to you anymore – town records upstairs, have a nice day."

A Kind of Drowning

Crowe climbed the staircase to the second floor. Rows of waist-high shelves spanned the wall. Perched above them hung the *Rosscarrig Art Group*'s paintings. A myriad of still lives, seaside sunsets and one superb study of a boat hung in pastel and acrylic hues. He slid past 'History' to the small corner table with a reading light and docking port for a laptop. The forlorn looking shelf of leather-bound town records offered little by way of the island. Two volumes contained a few old plans: sheep crofter cottages, the Martello tower and a seemingly long list of British owners before the Canadian Billionaire bought it in the late 1960's. It then seemed to have been forgotten about, as if the family had put its acquisition in a wall safe somewhere. Apart from caves on the northern side where seventeenth century smugglers had plied their trade, the island, like the town it was tied to seemed to have always been the bridesmaid, but never the bride.

Between the books a laminated triptych fell onto the floor. Crowe folded it out; *The Rocky Shore Trail* was the title. Opened out, it showed all the varieties of shore-life and flora of Ireland and The British Isles. Starfish, urchins, and crabs lined up in neat rows with seaweed and his gaze fell on *'varieties of samphires'*.

Rock Samphires. *found on the Eastern seaboard of Ireland. A salt-tolerant plant. Marsh Samphire grows on muddy sandy flats, like estuaries. Rock Samphire, less common, found only along cliffs...*

He looked at the photograph.

What he had collected along the shore during the search and sealed in a cigarette box, jammed in with the frozen pizzas didn't look like anything in the pamphlet. He turned it over. Nothing.

Cutts had said Rock Samphire. If anything, his need to get to the island intensified; as if another light had gone on in his dimmed consciousness. Thea's remains had traces of it. Inishcarrig didn't have a beach. It was sheer cliffs all around apart from the old stone jetty and slipway. Crowe pulled back down the last record he had skimmed and thumbed to the page with the image of the island coiled in soundings and indecipherable maritime numerals.

He ran his finger around the outline of the island - and then he spotted it.

A long thin line that joined Inishcarrig to Roscarrig. A causeway. A strip of sand.

A rat-run. A way to and from the mainland. He was certain now.

Crowe creased up the laminate and jammed it into the pocket of his cargo pants. Looking around, he tore out the page from the book.

He took the stairs two at a time, his lumbering gait reverberating around the library.

Clodagh looked up from her computer.

"Whatever it is, the answer is no," she said.

Crowe reached inside his fleece and from the top pocket of his shirt pulled out the folded page.

"You tore a page out of a library book? For fuck's sake, Crowe," she hissed.

"It was covered in dust. Hardly the end-of-the-world now is it?"

"I could have photocopied it for you. Jesus, you could have even photographed it?" she muttered.

"Phone's out of battery," lied Crowe.

He flattened out the page. Clodagh followed his finger,

"Is this a spit, or a causeway?" he asked.

"No idea," she replied, "I've never heard of anything like that and I've lived here most of my life,"

She held up the page.

"Maybe seasonal, spring tide or neap tide – lunar event?" continued Crowe.

"Maybe the fishermen would know?" she handed him back the page, "You can pay for the rebinding of the book, Crowe,"

"Send me the invoice. Is there some way to find this causeway? I'd like to try walking out to the island,"

"Good luck with that," replied Clodagh.

Crowe folded the page and stuck it in a pocket,

"I will pay you €200 if you take me out to the island. I will also buy you dinner," he said.

She hesitated, "Not out of a takeaway?"

"A sit-down, bottle of wine, replete with actual napkins, knives and forks. Coffee in a cup and saucer. Perhaps a digestif to ward off the food coma?"

"Tempting offer. Not much by that in this town. I do know somewhere though. Might want to shave, Crowe. Shower might help. Meet me at the boathouse at four-thirty tomorrow morning, the weather's settled for the next few days."

"Boathouse?"

With the beginnings of a smile, Clodagh drew on a lined A4 page directions to the boathouse from the library. She folded it neatly, creasing it down with her short, sharp nails. Crowe thought of them scraping his back. He quickly shelved the image away.

"I think there's a spare life jacket. I know another kayaker in the club who has a two-person sea kayak. I'll have to check with them. They're local so they can drop it there."

"Can I have your…?"

"No. Crowe. You cannot have my number."

"So, it's a lottery, then, the charter?"

"'Fraid so, cash up front. Kayak or no kayak. Four-thirty. No guarantees."

"As it's a lottery, I'll give you €100 to get out and the balance when we get back. See you at 4:30," said Crowe.

"Do you think you can get there?" smiled Clodagh,

"How hard can it be?" he replied.

20

The halogen lights of the boathouse burned, casting stark shadows across the old English stone. Despite the cold, he was sweating from the effort of dragging the yellow two-seater kayak out onto the jetty.

"Did you bring a change of clothes?" asked Clodagh.

Clipped to the aft was a plastic barrel, Clodagh threw a supermarket bag in, presumably with dry clothing. She sealed it with swift turns of the lid.

"Never thought of it," replied Crowe.

Over his fleece, Crowe's life jacket struggled with his bulk. He wore a warm woollen hat to offset the freezing thin discomfort of running shoes, socks, and cargo pants. He wedged himself into the front cockpit. Low down in the water in the long thin kayak, a primordial fear gripped him. Beyond the arc of the boathouse lights and the safety of the estuary were the depths of the open sea.

And pitch blackness.

Above them, the stars looked like diamonds strewn across a black velvet sky.

Clodagh slid an aluminium paddle to him,

"Don't let this fall overboard, they cost an absolute fortune. And almost impossible to get."

Crowe found the paddle's weight deceptive; it felt as light as a feather.

Clodagh continued, "Shaft, power face, back face. The power face is the side of the blade that goes in first and catches the water. We're going to do a few circles in the estuary to get a rhythm going, then when I say so we head out. I'm going to chant *'IN'* until we get it right."

A Kind of Drowning

After a few meandering circles and frequent clash of blades, they headed out to sea.

"Christ, you are terrible, Crowe," she muttered. He was a liability, she thought. She found herself having to adjust her stroke continually.

Crowe had questions. The embers in his mind's cavern had started firing up and remained burning, illuminating the shadows. Under his hat was the folded notebook. Wedged between his ear and the hat's elastic, was a pencil pared to two fine points at either end. His fear dissipated with every stroke of the paddle. Out of the estuary, the full force of the elements hit them. The kayak bobbed and dipped with every stroke as they aimed the pitching prow toward the looming black outline of Inishcarrig. The effort took his mind off the seawater leaking in around the cockpit's rubber skirt.

"Do you know where the jetty is?" he shouted over his shoulder. He doubted the kayak would survive being hurled against the sheer cliffs.

"Yes!" yelled Clodagh, "Aim for the left of the island."

A deep wave thrust the bow upwards at a steep angle and the kayak then plunged into the trough. Crowe's paddle slipped from his hand and for a moment, he thought it would slide into the depths. He grabbed the blade at the last moment like a juggler and after a pause, began paddling again.

"Do you want to stop?" yelled Clodagh.

"No," he replied.

He could feel the frigid seawater numbing his toes. He wanted desperately to turn back to feel the security of terra firma, but his instincts told him that somehow Thea had got on the island without anyone knowing.

"We can turn back," shouted Clodagh.

"No."

"If I think it's too risky, we're turning back, Crowe,"

"No," he shouted. He was wheezing like an old bellows and spat up phlegm in long rivulets over the side. His heart felt like it was going to burst out of his chest.

"I'm the one with the walkie-talkie and the wet suit, Crowe - you're on your own if we tip over,"

"You won't get your cash then?"

"It'd be worth it just to see you drown,"

Midway, they finally synched and began to make good time. Like Nubian galley slaves they powered their vessel through the peaks and troughs. Clodagh couldn't see over Crowe; she strained her neck to check direction.

The island drew closer. A thread of blue appeared on the horizon as the world turned toward the sun. The clouds danced and chased each other across the sky as the sea and the island took form. As the last of the stars burned away, they reached the jetty of Inishcarrig. The craft banged and scraped against the Napoleonic stone as they manoeuvred toward the slipway. Clodagh eased herself out first. Crowe almost threw everything overboard getting out. But somehow, pin-wheeling and stumbling, he kept his balance. They dragged the kayak up the slip and onto the jetty. Clodagh expertly lashed the kayak to the ancient, rusted moorings and opened the plastic barrel. She produced a flask and two protein bars. Crowe's shoulders were a fireworks of agony and his legs were shaking.

"Aloha from Inishcarrig," he muttered.

The flask contained hot black coffee with a heroic shot of brandy coursing through it. Not instant coffee, but something that had stewed on a hob. From his fleece, Crowe took out two cigarettes. He had to shake the BIC to get a modest flame. They smoked until the brandy and nicotine dulled the pain.

"I'm sure this island is connected by a spit at low tide," he said.

"Apart from the book you vandalised, it's not on any local charts," she replied.

He pondered, "It could be seasonal? A couple of times a year?"

"Possibly." Clodagh replied, "I've never taken a kayak out this far."

"Possibly is good, so,"

She stubbed out the cigarette, flicked the butt over the jetty and stood up.

"I've got you here, now what?"

"We walk," said Crowe.

"You walk, I'll wait," said Clodagh.

He opened out *The Rocky Shore Trail*. "I'm looking for rock samphire. By the way, I saw a helicopter land here a few weeks ago. Over that way."

"I saw it too, was it The Gardai or Air sea rescue? They practice manoeuvres here,"

"Nope. One of those fancy private ones. A Dauphin to be exact," he replied.

"There's rumours in the town that drugs are brought in from here?"

A Kind of Drowning

"On jet skis, big 4-strokes," said Crowe.

"Anything is possible," she replied.

In sloshing, flapping strides he clambered over the jetty wall and picked his way through the heather and gorse towards the Martello Tower.

Clodagh looked out across the channel to the mainland and closed her eyes wishing she had brought sunglasses. The sun felt warm upon her skin. She checked her Fitbit; it was 7.45am. She unzipped the top of her wetsuit and put on her T-shirt and fleece. Her cycle shorts offered some comfort from the chafing rubber. Tying the arms of the wetsuit around her waist, she took the last mouthful out of the flask. She thought about the return journey with growing dread; Crowe looked exhausted and clumsy paddling could drown them both. She spied a small bright blue fishing smack – *The Crystal Sea*, Ned Donovan's family, with a host of gulls in tow. From her fleece, she pulled out her mobile and rang it.

"It's Clodagh Robertson, Ned. Any chance of lift?" she asked.

"Are you in trouble, Clodagh?" his Dublin growl was warped with distortion,

"No Ned, my kayak got caught up with some dead weight. I'm at the jetty of Inishcarrig."

"Will two hours do?"

"See you then."

She sat at the edge, dangling her legs, staring down into the deep. Clodagh dialled Ned again,

"Ned. Clodagh again. I've a question for you…"

A Kind of Drowning

***

Crowe trudged toward the tower. He was sweating, he was cold, hot, and damp all at the same time. The area around the tower was fenced with pegs, fluttering pennants, and twine. Clearly marked out for development. Beyond was a flat expanse of land. The island was deceptively big and even. It had the picture postcard beauty of a property owned by an absentee landlord. Higher on one side, it swept downwards toward the Irish sea, the fields dotted with a few abandoned crofter's houses. A Georgian style manor house stood in faded glory. Crowe followed an old trail to the cliffs at the southern end of the island where the Martello Tower stood. Peering over the edge, amid the wild grasses, the trail continued. He slid down it slowly, his cheap soles offering little purchase. At any moment he expected to fall into the sea, but the trail meandered downwards. He clutched the grass; if he slipped, nothing would stop him sliding helter-skelter off the edge. He removed his shoes and socks, draping them on a rock. The feeling of wet grass between his toes revived his flagging muscles. Over another slight rise and Crowe found himself in a V-shaped cove, masked on both sides by rocks with a thin stretch of soft sand no wider than a few yards. It felt warm beneath his heels. He walked to the water's edge.

Shaking out a cigarette Crowe lit it. Taking his folded jotter out from under his hat, he noted the time from his phone and drew a crude sketch. The waves slid closer, then as they ebbed, he saw it. Just below the surface a line of sand continued out to sea. It had to be the spit. His eyes followed it out, the mainland was much closer this side. The Martello would have been manned under British rule. In his mind's eye, he pictured men in tricorn hats and laden mules wading across at low tide to keep the tower maintained with firewood and provisions.

He stepped out into the sea. The sand was firm underfoot and he inched out. The water depth didn't change for several yards. He waded up to his knees without the sand giving way from under him. The sunlight dappled his shins and toes. The spit slid into darker waters a few feet either side of him. He turned and walked back. On the small stretch of sand, he looked up and down several times. The coffee was acting as a diuretic, he needed to piss. He looked around and unzipped. As he urinated, he looked slowly around the small shoreline.

He spotted something on an outcrop.

Zipping up, he reached for *The Rocky Shore Trail*. Opening it out he knew what he was looking at. The samphire grew all over the rocks in dense clumps. He tossed his cigarettes out of the box and looking around, selected a few samples.

"You're a nineteen-year-old girl, fit, able and knowledgeable," he muttered, "you sneak here and then what…?"

He wended his way back up the trail, gathering up his sodden socks and runners. He pulled them on and gingerly ascended the incline. The gradient was steep and about forty feet to the top.

Higher than anything along the beach of Roscarrig, he thought. He stopped and looked back out at the sea. It shimmered in the spring light. Then turning back something silver and shiny caught the sunlight.

A long thin tube. Crowe picked it up.

It was a cigar holder. The text was faded along the seal –
LONS _ _ _ E.

He was about to toss it back, but some inner voice told him that it didn't belong here on this island, so if it didn't belong here…

"What are you doing here?" he asked it.

He twisted the top. Then stopped. If it was evidence, he knew he had compromised it. The tube wasn't rusted or damaged or exposed to the elements for long. He pocketed it. Crowe panned around, his senses hunted for echoes, subtle hints of events. Something happened out here on this desolate rock. Knowing something and proving it were two completely different things.

He stowed away the cigar tube.

He made his way more cautiously, stopping at the tower. The remains of a building lay strewn around it. He climbed up onto the ruined wall. There from a slightly higher vantage point, he could see two long lines in the grass.

Helicopter skids.

A cigar tube, a helicopter and Thea Farrell drowned. His eyes flicked expertly, looking for hidden traces, flattened grass, divots, something to indicate a disturbance. Someone had held the cigar tube and dropped it recently. He circled slowly around, the grasses were high and danced in the breeze. They were wet from the early morning dew.

Mr. Grumpy Thea had called him. Whoever did this to her was about to find out how fucking grumpy he could get. The evidence, as Cutts said, all pointed to an accident. But this felt, *smelled* like a crime scene. The end of Thea's life began here. At this place.

His thoughts were broken as he spotted Clodagh walking towards him. Her strides were assured. The wetsuit wrapped around her waist and her hair tied up gave her a boyish shape.

"Just spoke to a local fisherman, Ned Donovan," she said, "there's a spit alright, only crossable four times a year at the strongest spring tides. The sea is only a few inches deep when that happens, but it fills up fast," she said, "the last one was four weeks ago,"

Her breathing was measured as she stood beside him letting the sentence hang. A flash of freckles dashed across her nose and forehead. Faint smoker's lines around her mouth faded in her grin.

"It's over there," pointed Crowe.

21

Donovan's boat brought them close to the estuary mouth. As Clodagh was lowered into the kayak, she told Crowe she'd manage better without him,

"I'll give you the balance tonight," he said.

"See you for dinner," she said lashing his paddle to the kayak.

"I haven't booked…?" he started.

"I have. Meet me at the library at five sharp. Shave, and a pair of pants would be nice."

"Can't guarantee it," he said.

"Don't stand me up, John, I mean it."

As she rowed away, Crowe wanted her to look back, perhaps acknowledge with some secret smile that for a few hours that morning, they had shared an adventure. But she didn't.

Donovan's rusted and sturdy vessel churned its way out of the shallows back into the channel. Crowe checked his watch, but he didn't have a watch. He reached for a cigarette behind his ear, but he didn't have one,

"Were you part of the search for Thea Farrell?" he asked.

"I was. It's a shame about how it ended," said Donovan. He shook a cigarette packet out of his oil-stained overalls and offered them to Crowe.

As he prised one out, Crowe could see the faded pink from under Donovan's hat.

"Thanks for the lift, it's very much appreciated. Do you know the Farrells well?" said Crowe.

"We're a close-knit community out here. There are two types of family – old Roscarrig and new – their families are old. Clodagh's one of our own. So was Thea. What about you?"

Donovan was a leathery cadaver of a man, but as solid and reliable as the battered looking wheelhouse.

"Just passing through," replied Crowe, "So Thea's parents' are Roscarrig natives too?"

"Yup, both – went to school together, local childhood sweethearts. Andrew could have made it to the senior panel. Great lár na páirce. No one could catch him on a run, future Dublin captain, if only he could have controlled that Farrell temper,"

"What happened?"

"Red mist. Broke another player's jaw. Deliberately. Short fuse that family, same with the father. Tough bastards the lot of them. Fancy a brew?"

"Thanks, yes."

Crowe watched Donovan amble over to the wheelhouse. Seagulls whirled overhead hoping for scraps, their shrieks primordial and threatening. Crowe thought of their ruthlessness when they plucked out Thea's eyes. He looked back at the island. It shone and seemed much closer, a trick of the atmospherics.

Donovan emerged with two metal mugs from the wheelhouse and handed one to Crowe. It was tea as Crowe's father used to say, you could walk on. A milky looking tar.

After the morning exertions, it tasted like an angel's kiss.

"The tide was kind today," said Donovan.

Crowe nodded out toward the island.

A Kind of Drowning

"Are drownings common?" he asked,

"More than you think. That outcrop over there is known as 'suicide point'. Local kids go tombstoning off it in the summer."

"How do they get out there?" asked Crowe.

He shaded his eyes against the glare of the sea. Donovan's long weather beaten index finger pointed out to the island, close to where Crowe had found the cove.

"Paddle boards, some go windsurfing, some even swim it," he said.

"Jet Skis?" asked Crowe,

"If you're mad enough, yeah,"

"I saw a helicopter land there the other day; not Air / Sea Rescue," said Crowe.

"Lots of comings and goings over the past few months. There's an old smuggler's cove on the far side. Some of the local families used to run tea over to England for the black market during the Second World War. I've heard rumours drugs are coming in through it now. The sooner its sold, the better."

Crowe studied the shoreline around Roscarrig; there were literally hundreds of small beaches and hidden coves that could accommodate a narcotics shipment.

And this far out from the city, not enough Guards.

"Growing town, growing demand," said Crowe.

"There are rumours of a top dog in the drugs game living on the outskirts of the town." nodded Donovan.

"You never know who's moved in beside you," said Crowe.

"'True," said Donovan, "this town loves its rumours,"

They leaned against the gunwale smoking and watching the coast slide by. Crowe thought about Quigley, wondering what part of the town he had gone to when warning Teflon D.

"Thea was local, she'd have known the sea around these parts?" said Crowe.

"Air/Sea Rescue should send this town Christmas cards the amount of overtime we give them. This time of year, the tide can catch you unawares. Even the seasoned fishermen get caught in it. You get these city types coming down for the weekend doing kite surfing and wind surfing. Wrong time of the day or week and the next stop is Wales. There's a deep channel north of the island, acts like a sort of tunnel when it surges – a killer."

Crowe thought of Thea propelled underwater, dead. Battered and torn before she rose again and was delivered into the crowded harbour.

"Anything like shoes or clothing come up in those nets?"

"Hauled a FIAT 127 up once, but no; clothing usually disintegrates or sinks. Shoes would probably slip through the nets. I recognised you the moment I saw you - you're that Guard who was all over the news and the internet?"

"Yep. Laying low,"

"Red mist."

"I'm calmer now,"

"Old habits."

"Old habits," replied Crowe, "If a ladies Nike runner, size 4 ever surfaces?"

"I'll let Clodagh know – does she have your number?"

A Kind of Drowning

"She had my number a while ago,"

Donovan tilted back his cap and laughed. It sounded like something from the grave.

"Smart girl, like her mother – would buy and sell you before you knew what was happening," he said.

The harbour came into view and once the boat had moored, Crowe hauled himself up the ancient metal ladder to the top. He ached from the exercise and felt unexpectedly queasy and exhausted. He wondered if Gallaher was on one of his extended lunches.

Crowe looked around for the Lexus hoping to catch a lift.

Across the road and chained to the bollards that lined the pavement, a bicycle caught his eye. It was a white, thin, expensive looking one shining in the sunlight. The doors of the Boogie-Woogie flashed the sun as they swung open and a man in his mid-twenties dressed in upmarket athleisure unlocked the bike. The windshell hoodie was a vivid orange as were the running shoes. A baseball cap was perched jauntily on his head. He straddled the bike lithely and swinging out onto the road, pedalled no-handed sipping from a disposable coffee-cup. The man's insouciance jarred like a photo-fit against the downbeat collection of buildings, vans, and cars.

Like Crowe, he didn't belong in Roscarrig.

A student type Karen at the bookies had said. Crowe dug out his phone and dialled,

"Derry? Its John. Fancy a jaunt to the big smoke?"

Gallagher wheezed into the phone, "Is it important, John?"

"Very. Life or death. Can you pick me up at the apartment in thirty minutes?"

"Sure, why not? I'll clear my appointments and tell Hilary to hold my calls,"

Crowe fought the urge to laugh, "I also need two hundred from the money belt. And while you're there; I need a padded envelope, a black marker, and compliments slip,"

Crowe set out on foot, following the free-wheeling cyclist. At the T junction into the town, Crowe ducked up and across the side streets that acted as a short-cut to the betting shop.

He wasn't disappointed.

"Got a light, bud?" Crowe asked, waving a cigarette

The cyclist was just pushing the bike through the betting shop door. Though he was momentarily wrong-footed, he merely glanced at the profusely sweating and wheezing Crowe.

"No. I don't smoke," he replied, "those things will kill you, you know,"

With a shove, he forced the bike through. Up close, Crowe was right; this guy was too shiny and new like a cigar holder for this town and his voice was Southside educated Dublin.

"Thanks for that," replied Crowe, "How's your boss these days?"

"Boss?" replied the man nonplussed.

"The one missing the thumb? Teflon?"

Crowe wasn't sure but he thought the cyclist had blushed, he was still young enough to.

As the cyclist shouldered and disappeared through the narrow door he said, "Fuck off and stop annoying me. Go panhandle somewhere else,"

A Kind of Drowning

Taking the stairs two at a time to the garret, Crowe undressed in the apartment, towelled himself quickly and changed into clean tee, black fleece, and sweatpants. He dug out two odd socks from the laundry basket and donned his spare running shoes. He photographed his make-shift case board and sent the image to Cutts' phone.

He pulled on a plain baseball cap and from behind the door, a Hi-Viz he had borrowed from the storeroom in the local supermarket. Standing at the mirror in the bathroom, he studied himself.

Dressed in black, with a Day-Glo vest he looked like a courier.

His eyes drifted toward the S-bend, to where the twist of coke was hidden. And it dawned on him - the cigar holder. He went back to the kitchen table and pulling on a pair of marigolds, he twisted the top off. Holding the tube up to the light, he could see something wound up inside the tube. Giving it a tap at the end, he watched a few grains of white powder fall onto the table along with a $100 bill.

Cocaine. Pure top-grade el-supremo cocaine. It tingled on his gums.

He put everything back together and wrapped it up in cling film. He tried Cutts' phone one more time. It went to messaging.

He glanced up at the cup and saucer clock – time to go.

The Lexus was idling outside. Gallagher's boom-box voice was hollering into his mobile. Crowe slid into the passenger side. Without pausing for breath, Gallaher handed over a huge envelope and marker pen.

In the A3 padded envelope Crowe slotted in the samphire in the cigarette box, a written note with the location and the cigar tube. Next in was *The Rocky Shore Trail*. On the front of the A3, he scrawled: *F.A.O. Dr. Olivia Cutts. Assistant State Pathologist C/O Forensics, Garda HQ.*

On the reverse of the envelope, he scrawled *'MERMAID'*.

"Can I put the hazards on?" asked Derry, hanging up.

"No," replied Crowe. Looking at the clock on the dashboard he said, "I need to be at the library by five pm,"

"Then we'd better put the pedal to the metal, John."

"Try not to get us pulled over,"

Gallagher tapped the media player screen and Barry Manilow blared out through the speakers.

What was worse is that Derry Gallagher thought he could sing.

It was going to be a long, long drive.

22

Crowe watched Clodagh cycle towards the library. The late afternoon sunset was the perfect backdrop for her arrival. The bone-cutting breeze drifted in from the coast winding its way under Crowe's jacket and shirt. His jeans had refused to grow with his girth, and its waistband sliced into him.

"Well worth the wait," he said.

"You're on time," she replied.

Clodagh dismounted and secured the bike to the library fence. Her jeans and top looked stylish and brand new. A striking amber pendant and an ornate bracelet were the only adornments. In a flat heel, she was eye level with him. Her make-up was subtle, her perfume too.

"You scrub up pretty well, yourself," she replied.

He'd shaved for the first time in a week, lathering up his head as well. Just as he started into the left side of his head the bathroom lights had suddenly gone out. The ensuing cut was covered up with his hat. Patched in balm and toilet paper, the wound pounded mercilessly.

"Are power cuts frequent around here?" he asked.

"They don't happen too often. There's a substation close to the harbour, just all the new homes coming on stream creates a spike in demand. Christmas Day last year was down for the whole day. It should be back in a few hours – why, were you thinking of bailing on me?"

His body, unused to the level of exercise that morning already felt like it had been fed through a wringer.

"Not at all, I thought you'd arrive in a taxi?"

"It's a fifteen-minute walk, Crowe. Even you can manage that?"

"Is there a short cut?" he replied.

"I think you need the exercise; that jacket looks a little snug."

"Just a little tight at the shoulders, maybe,"

"Yeah, right," she grinned.

They cut across the library grounds away from the coast, through a housing estate that looked desolate in the half-light. After a series of side roads, they found themselves walking along a long boreen. Both sides were lined with unruly hedgerows that forced them at times into single file. The shelter cocooned them from the coastal wind but drew the shadows closer about them. Clodagh's strides were long, Crowe struggled to keep up with her pace. His stomach growled in protest.

"You made it back to the boathouse, ok?" he asked

"Without all the dead-weight? Yep," she replied.

"Hilarious. How did you get the yellow thing back on its trailer?"

"The 'Thing' is called a kayak and I had help," she replied .

"Help?"

"There were more rowers out and about – plenty of offers,"

"I'll bet," said Crowe.

Clodagh smiled to herself that Crowe had a tinge of jealousy about him,

"I see Derry was closed for the afternoon?" she said.

"He gave me a lift," replied Crowe.

"Anywhere exciting?"

"Garda HQ," said Crowe, "I think it broke the drudgery of his day. He wanted to put the hazards on, break the speed limit and use the bus lanes."

"Dragooning poor old Derry, shame on you, Crowe. I hope you were delivering a letter of apology, taking responsibility for your assault? I had a look at the footage on YouTube, you do realise you nearly killed a man?"

"No and no - I had to submit some theories, ideas…"

"The Island? Thea?" she said.

"Yes. On paper, Thea had an accident, Clodagh."

"On paper? The way you say that you think otherwise?"

"I do. I think something happened to her. I think, and it's only a hunch, she was in the wrong place at the wrong time resulting in her death."

Clodagh stopped. She had been walking a few paces ahead and turned toward him. He stared directly at Clodagh. He needed her to listen to him. He needed some reaction, some validation.

"Who would hurt her? Why, Crowe? She was just a kid," said Clodagh.

"I don't know, Clodagh. I threw my eye around the area near the tower. You get a 'feel' for a spot. I think she was there. I don't know why, but I think I know how. She crossed the spit, she may have had to wade; which begs the question, why would she go to her bolthole, a secret place in the middle of the night? Maybe she'd run away from something and went head first into something worse. Even if she'd been caught by the tide, she would have been well capable of making it to shore."

A Kind of Drowning

Clodagh stood facing him in the fading light, her slightly square face, framed in shoulder length hair gave her an androgynous appearance. Her eyes glittered in the half-light in concern.

"That's terrible, I mean it, Crowe – even to think that way?"

"I have to ask you, just out of curiosity, Andrew Farrell, the father, any gossip?"

"Gossip. Seriously?"

"Prone to 'red mist'…?"

"Pot calling kettle? No, I haven't heard any 'gossip' as you call it. All I've heard is that he's a good man, very attentive to her and Grace. A pillar of the community."

A man, Crowe's father would have labelled as 'a man of consequence'.

"Was he resentful of Thea's achievements? The mother seemed to blame him in the church,"

"No, Crowe. He was grieving…Grace was grieving - Christ, show some fucking compassion."

"Let's not ruin the evening, shall we? I've sent in my concerns, but only as a private citizen, Clodagh," he said, "I'm persona non grata these days, anyway. It'll wind up in a tray somewhere, but I feel I've fought her corner,"

"Or re-opened old wounds, Crowe. A hunch isn't a fact."

"Once a cop, always a cop, it's a bad habit," replied Crowe.

"Then it's easy to see why you're on your own,"

She turned on her heel and shouted over her shoulder,

"How can you live with yourself, Crowe? Seriously?"

A Kind of Drowning

Well, the evening's going just swimmingly, thought Crowe.

The narrow laneway gave way to a main road. They crossed it in silence.

"Here we are," she said.

It was a large, thatched pub called 'The Coachman'. Every window was lit by candle light. Protected by pine and yew trees, it glowed softly in the gloom.

"Now this looks like a hidden gem. I didn't think a place like this existed," said Crowe.

"Local knowledge, Crowe. Its nearly two hundred years old and an early house too."

"Good to know," replied Crowe, "Maybe we should have a liquid breakfast here? I hate to eat on an empty stomach - what time does it open at?"

"Five-thirty, so the fisherman can have a few before they put out to sea. The road leads down to the harbour, you could walk to it in ten minutes."

Clodagh held the door open for Crowe. Inside, every table was lit with candles and tea lights in multicoloured glass. The bar's mirror, chipped and faded in places, reflected the light in prisms of amber flame. A turf fire glowed and smouldered from an antique hearth, the ingles and pans seared in black.

A waitress checked the booking in a large A4 desk diary using the torch on her phone. She drew a highlighter across their names,

"Hi Clodagh, thanks for that recommendation, I hope to have the book back by next weekend," she said.

"Take your time, Aoife. There's no penalty these days, I'm glad you're enjoying Garcia Marquez, he's a great writer."

A Kind of Drowning

"*Love in the Time of Cholera* is pretty apt for these days too, Clodagh," said Aoife,

Crowe noticed the hand sanitiser dispenser beside the diary. Aoife pumped it a few times into her hands before reaching for two menus. He had also noted her double take at the pair of them. She guided them to their table. From her smart shirt and waistcoat, Aoife oozed efficiency.

"We've no electricity, but the gas is working, so everything on the menu should be ok. Only thing is, the card machine isn't working," said Aoife.

"I have cash," said Crowe.

"That's great, guys. Just to let you know the beer taps are down too and the blackout has affected the wine coolers," said Aoife, "so it's bottled ale or we can serve the house red,"

"Do you have whiskey?" asked Crowe

"Yes, we do though ice is limited, we sent one of the lads out to get some from the nearest hotel," said Aoife.

"I'll have a whiskey, single malt if possible, no ice please, por favor – Clodagh?"

"Tap water," she replied flatly.

He knew he should have invited her to choose first; how long was it since he'd been on a date? Twenty years? What was the etiquette? Was this even a date?

Crowe began to sweat. The table felt suddenly small.

He felt somehow he'd missed a cue.

"How are the chefs coping?" asked Clodagh, with a smile that seemed painted on.

A Kind of Drowning

"They all have head torches; the kitchen is like a coal mine in there. I'll get the drinks and give you time to choose," replied Aoife.

Lauren and Lucy at The Boogie-Woogie should study her, as she was the complete opposite to them, thought Crowe. No visible ink, no attitude, just smiles. He looked around; the restaurant was only half full. Mostly couples, but no families.

They both selected steak, vegetables, and fries from the menu. Crowe ordered two glasses of red. Clodagh asked for a blue steak, Crowe for well done.

Aoife returned with the wine. Crowe gulped it down, Clodagh sipped. Crowe couldn't put his finger on it, but he felt Aoife was staring at him.

"I'll have another whiskey, same again, Jameson. No ice,"

Aoife looked at Clodagh who smiled a no-thanks. Another diner called over to her and she briskly dealt with their question.

Too sharp for this town, thought Crowe.

"You can take your hat off," said Clodagh

"Not advisable," said Crowe, "I dabbled with shaving my head, it didn't go so well. Might put you off your steak. So, do you enjoy working in the library?"

Clodagh shifted slightly in her chair. Crowe had an intensity about him, something missing from his first visit at the library had been found. Like he'd just plugged himself back in. His gaze could be warm and yet destructive if need be,

"It gives me a place to write poetry," she said.

"Have you had anything published?" he asked.

"No,"

"Why not?"

Clodagh stared at him for a moment and shrugged.

"I'd fret over every word, they'd never be good enough,"

"There's a lot of crap out there, these days, you should do it anyway?"

"Why would I do that, Crowe?"

Her eyes were a deep green. He hadn't noticed this before. Not quite aqua marine, the colour reminded him of the sea. They too had treacherous depths. Maybe it was part of his recovery, an improving awareness of things around him? He'd begun to see things in sharp relief, like an incremental adjustment to a pair of binoculars.

"Ah, the tortured poet, I get it. What about before you became a librarian?" he asked.

"I worked in a supermarket. It started as a part-time job when I was at school. Then I worked at the check-out and eventually became the manager. I married my childhood sweetheart, wanted to be a mother, have lots of kids, you know, the suburban housewife dream. It didn't work out."

A haunted look flashed across her eyes, briefly, then it was gone.

"Then I took a degree at Queens University, Belfast, and the option to study as a librarian got me placed in Roscarrig, back home with my mother. She has dementia. That's it, I'm afraid," she said.

The carafe of water arrived. Crowe poured for Clodagh.

"So, how did you become interested in rowing?" asked Crowe.

"Kayaking. Because living was becoming a drag…"

Clodagh suddenly needed a vodka and a cigarette. She fidgeted with the cutlery,

"It's either GAA in this town, rowing, kayaking or sit at home. I had some money from the divorce settlement, took lessons and bought my kayak. Roscarrig Rowing Club can be a bunch of fanatics, I just needed some piece of mind, some alone time. The kayak suits my needs."

"You rowed really well," said Crowe.

"You need more practice," replied Clodagh, "You nearly tipped us over,"

"Maybe I'll try again," replied Crowe, "But thank you for giving me something I had never done before,"

"Did you enjoy it?"

"Once the sheer fucking terror died down, yes. Yes, I enjoyed it."

It won him a hard-earned smile.

The silence lengthened. They found things to look at. Things to file for small conversation. Things that would never be said. The evening felt over before it had begun. Crowe longed to loosen his belt; he felt the circulation around his hips slowing down. He prayed that deep vein thrombosis would end this evening.

The meals arrived. Clodagh's steak bled into the steamed vegetables as she cut it, Crowe's looked like it hadn't survived a nuclear blast.

"How's that cremation you're sawing into?" she asked,

"Perfect."

Crowe mashed some fries into his mouth and downed the whiskey, he motioned for another.

Clodagh chewed slowly through the drawn-out silence,

"Can you order me one as well?"

Crowe held up a second finger, Aoife nodded.

"So, Crowe, what about you?" asked Clodagh.

"If you saw me on YouTube, then there's really not much more to tell," said Crowe. So, long story, short – I went to Belvedere College, but got expelled…"

"Don't tell me, a problem with authority?" said Clodagh

"Yep, the Jesuits turfed me out for arson as well as disciplinary issues. Blackrock College took me in, then Trinity and then I enrolled in the Gardai," he continued.

"A silver spoon and the world at your feet, and you become a Guard?"

"Family tradition, I'm afraid," said Crowe, "My Father and Grandfather. It was expected that I get my head out of the clouds, or *out of my arse* as dad would say and start earning a living."

"Weight of expectation?"

Crowe sensed a sudden interest. A shift in the mood between them, maybe the growing thrombosis around the waistband could wait.

"The plight of the only child. Got my degree in Sciences and Philosophy and then signed up," he said.

"Your marriage?" asked Clodagh

"Over. In truth it's been over for years. This has been hard on my son Cathal. You may have recognised him in the footage as the boy who wanted the ground to swallow him up."

"How old is he?"

"Fifteen, well, nearly fifteen."

Crowe motioned to another passing waitress for a refill, her reaction was more like Lauren.

The whiskeys glowed in the candle light, Clodagh downed hers in one. They finished their meal.

"Tell you what, why don't we order a bottle of red and some coffees?" suggested Crowe.

"Good idea," replied Clodagh.

She took in the room, the wooden panels, the old tables, and pictures on the wall. Perhaps she had misread the situation. The evening had been awkward; Crowe had a habit of riling a person, getting under their skin. But wasn't that the sign of a good policeman? The ability to make you take a wrong step?

It wasn't quite disappointment, but a certain hollowness to the evening that gnawed on Clodagh. A sense of anti-climax.

"So why Andrew Farrell?" she had lowered her voice.

"Derry's not subtle. He implied, I stress, *implied* that Andrew Farrell seemed relieved when they recovered Thea's body."

"He had got his daughter back. Dead, that's true, but in one piece. The seas around here aren't always so forgiving. As for Derry, he loves his dramas. Everyone in the town knows he courted Grace before she set her sights on Andrew,"

"Did he ever marry?"

"No. Grace broke his heart."

"You know this how?"

"Before she went to pieces, my mother was the jungle telegraph. She was an old school curtain twitcher. So how do you know Derry?"

Aoife hovered before setting down two big wine glasses. With an expert twist, she removed the cork and smelled it. Crowe noticed she had deep dimples when she smiled. Crowe indicated Clodagh take a sip. Aoife poured an exact measure without spilling a drop. Clodagh smelled, swirled, and tasted – she smiled back,

"Thanks, Aoife, perfect,"

Aoife poured two exact measures and placed the bottle in the middle between them. The evening had tilted from crisis into smooth waters, thought Crowe.

"In answer to your question; Derry is my landlord."

"How did that happen?"

"A mutual acquaintance,"

"So, why Andrew?" she repeated, "There are plenty more morons in this town, deadbeats, wife-beaters, wasters and no-hopers."

"If Thea was killed you have to look at those closest to her first. Andrew has some of the characteristics of a domestic abuser."

"You are very, very much off the mark, Crowe,"

And there it was, the tightening of the air around Clodagh. The set of the jaw, the look in her eyes, the sense of tribal loyalty.

"Maybe you're right, Clodagh."

As he reached for the bottle to pour, a sudden twitch, a sudden muscular spasm ran the length of his arm. He swiped more than grabbed the bottle and knocked it and its contents onto Clodagh. It glugged out a huge amount of wine.

A Kind of Drowning

"Jesus, Crowe," she said.

He stood to lean over with a napkin and tilted the table with his weight. The plate, the glasses and the bottle crashed around her like artillery fire.

Aoife was across in an instant.

Everyone turned and stared.

If this had been the wild west, thought Crowe as he blushed to his cut-up shaven scalp – even the piano player would have stopped.

"No, Crowe. No. Just fuck right off – now," hissed Clodagh.

He leaned on the bar peeling off the Euros and settling the bill. Aoife had tidied up the mess and Clodagh had stormed past him to the toilets without making eye contact.

Aoife stood at the open cash register with a funeral stare,

"Think I'll get a second date?" he asked.

"I genuinely doubt it," she replied.

"Hope springs eternal - keep the change," he said.

As an afterthought he handed her a fifty,

"Order a taxi for Clodagh, please."

Just over Aoife's shoulder he could see a framed picture. It was Casey Clarke and Ephraim Hunt frozen in the moment of pulling pints for the locals. Caught in the flash, Hunt without the trademark sunglasses resembled a mashed up Elvis,

"All the celebs, I see," he said.

Aoife glanced over her shoulder,

"She's lovely, he's a dickhead. They've a house on the coast road; the old vicarage,"

"Farandore or Dublin direction?" asked Crowe

"Farandore," she replied.

He'd pay Derry Gallagher a visit tomorrow.

"Ever have an out-of-towner here? A man about my age with a missing thumb?"

"We get all sorts here. But nothing springs to mind,"

Crowe left to the pitying gaze of the diners and found himself looking up and down the road.

Which way was it to the harbour? he thought.

He trudged in the wrong direction.

***

Aoife made a commiserate smile as Clodagh came back,

"I can arrange a sambuca and a coffee on the house?" she said

"Can I change that to a double vodka?" said Clodagh

"After him? No problem. I'll phone a taxi; he's paid for it."

Aoife turned to Clodagh and smiled,

"The taxi will be here in ten," she said.

23

From the edge of the jetty where he sat, Crowe could see a lone Jet ski flitting out in the channel. He was still smarting at the previous night's debacle and sipped a double espresso with his cigarette. The jet-ski buzzed past the net buoys and on the calm sea, left a trailing V in its wake. It pitched and buffeted its way toward Inishcarrig, then banked suddenly eastwards, making a sharp right-angle running parallel to the coast.

Crowe trudged down toward the beach and then walked along it, tracking the jet ski's progress.

The jet ski disappeared around the headland. The tide was out, allowing Crowe to pick his way across the shale and rocks to the far side. It led to the public car park not far from where Teflon D had walked the dog. Derry was right; midweek, Roscarrig was nothing but a ghost town. The beach was completely deserted. As Crowe rounded the rocks, he could see the empty car park. Zephyrs of warm sand spun across it like tiny tornadoes, hoovering up pieces of litter as they went. Adjacent to the car park was an old weather beaten slipway, darkened, smoothed and green from exposure to the elements. Parked along it was a brand new smoked glass Mercedes SUV; a top-of-the-range muscle machine. Lower down, closer to the water's edge, a man was securing the jet ski to a trailer. He stood up and reached for a tarpaulin crumpled near the vehicle. In profile, Crowe had no doubt; it was one of Teflon D's mini-me's, two branches of the same fucked-up, coke-addled dynasty. Finding him alone offered Crowe an advantage. He climbed the sand to the car park, crossed it and stood at the top of the slipway looking down. In the heat, Crowe could smell sweat, seawater and rubber coming off the man. Even with the neoprene, life preserver and helmet, Teflon junior wasn't your average boy band fodder. Each hand was heavily tattooed and adorned with rings inset with black and aqua marine stones. Crowe recognised cheap knuckle dusters when he saw them. But what would Crowe know about the current music scene?

Junior loped off up the slipway and activated the hitch. The trailer inched up toward the Merc.

The mini-me's mobile rang and he answered. Some joke was cracked down the line and his high-pitched hyena giggle magpied its way around the slipway.

Crowe didn't think any niceties were required,

"Where's your other half?" he asked.

The mini-me spun looking left and right, but not behind him.

"Setanta Cosgrave isn't it?" said Crowe

"I'm Fionn," he looked back. Then returned to his phone call. The giggling had evolved into a snorting gasp.

Fionn ended the call and ignored Crowe.

"Hi, Fionn. That jet ski there. How far does one of those things go on a tank of petrol? What's its operational range?" said Crowe stepping closer. As Fionn wrestled the tarp over the dripping jet ski, Crowe could see it was a big machine, a 4-stroke probably. A glistening mighty pachyderm of the waves.

Fionn fastened down the tarp with tight, spasmic pulls. He looked from side-to-side, not making eye contact. His eyes looked glassy, but it could have been the exposure to the elements and sea water.

"Bet it could make it to the island and back, no bother. Were you there just now? Were you there at night a few weeks ago?" said Crowe

Fionn Cosgrave froze, blinking at the questions. Long enough for Crowe to step closer. Like a prize fighter spotting a gap in the opponent's technique, Crowe gambled on the fact that the scion of a

Dublin gangster wasn't used to any old Joe Public talking to him this way,

"Were you on the island two weeks ago when Thea Farrell disappeared? Lovely girl, tough, a real battler, vulnerable though, wouldn't you agree?" Crowe pressed.

"I've *nooo* idea what you're talking about, pal," replied Fionn.

He was getting agitated. He had a sort of Dublin-mid-Atlantic accent, a Bob Geldof with the flu,

"So, Fionn where's the other half, Setanta? I usually see the pair of you out in the channel?" said Crowe, "Faffing about, making a nuisance of yourselves. Is he on the island now? That trailer looks like it could take two of those things."

Fionn stopped and looked at Crowe. He began to pull himself together, that little sprinkling of showbiz appeared. The beginnings of a sneer touched the side of his mouth,

"Lost your way from the homeless shelter, have you?" he said, "I'd give you some change for the bus, only I really couldn't give a fuck,"

He shrugged off his life preserver and peeled down the neoprene. His body was oddly hairless and festooned in a kaleidoscope of tattoos. Folds of gathering fat were early signs of a body going to seed amid the youthful muscle. Crowe vaguely remembered the twins had a dance routine on the TV. One that involved leaping about and performing hand stands. He remembered Harris' comments about the Garda National Drugs Unit and INTERPOL, but something about Fionn's attitude and stance worked its way under Crowe's skin. The sense of entitlement achieved on the back of other people's misery and pain. A top of the range luxury vehicle just sitting there like a pristine toddler's tricycle. Another disposable plaything. He thought of the gulf between this pup's wealth and his own years of slog with a state pension at the end; not even small change to this clown.

"I heard your Beemer got burned. Must have affected the old image?" said Crowe.

It got the response he'd been needling for,

"Go fuck yourself, you fat hobo. Try using soap, I can smell you from here,"

The snarl turned to a sneer, Fionn giggled to himself in little yips.

Crowe stepped forward.

"I care about what happened to Thea. If I find you or the other knuckle dragger had anything to do with it…" said Crowe.

"You'll what? Look pal, no one really cares about some ugly retard. You look like one of them; by the looks of it I'd say you can barely dress yourself, retard," said Fionn.

The trailer was at the tow bar and Fionn hoisted it into place, securing it. He looked around the beach and car park with jerky nods. His wet peroxided hair resembled a coxcomb.

"I have no fucking idea what you're talking about, now fuck off, old man," he said as an afterthought.

Crowe pulled out his crumpled cigarette box and lighter. He thought about the cigarette smouldering on the end of Grace Farrell's lips, spilling ash onto a grimy kitchen table.

"I'd offer you one, but it's the last one," said Crowe shaking the lighter for a spark,

"Hope you get emphysema," leered Fionn.

A Kind of Drowning

"Her name was Thea, Fionn. Thea. Farrell. This young woman dies; it's in all the papers, all over social media and you shrug. Mention your damaged car, Fionn, and you have an embolism. Is Desmond Cosgrave your dad? The one a Chinaman once mutilated? Heard they made him walk to the hospital. Imagine that – your fucking thumb at the bottom of the Royal Canal. That kind of makes you psycho, resentful, kind of makes you want to hurt people, lash out at the injustice of it all. Hurt vulnerable women. Easy targets for all that rage,"

Fionn was now pacing up and down the slip way. He was agitated, to Crowe, he resembled a farm animal trying to do algebra,

"Fuck you. FUCK YOU. Do you know who my Da is? Do you know who he is? Who I am? Do you know who you are dealing with, bud? He's the undisputed fucking heavyweight king of Dublin. The king. K-I-N-G of Ireland. We could do you, pal. Oh yeah, do you so they'd fucking cremate you out of pity because there'd be fuck all left to examine on the slab. And you wouldn't be missed, just another homeless loser!"

Crowe knew when a man was at his limits of control. Fionn was wired tight and about to go ape. His temples had coils appearing and the corneas around the eyes were turning red even from where Crowe stood. He lurched forward and in one smooth movement, gripped Fionn by the shoulders, spinning him faceward into the merc's side with a satisfying crunch of skull on metal. Crowe kicked Fionn's legs wide and wrenched the wrists back and up, immobilising him in a policeman's grip.

"Didn't your parents teach you to show some respect for your elders?" hissed Crowe. Then in one movement swung on his heels, throwing Fionn off the slipway.

Junior hit the sand face-first.

"They say Setanta is the brains of the band? I can see that from here. Was he on the island with your dad?" said Crowe, "Is that what happened to Thea? Ran into you three animals?"

"I know you," said Fionn looking up after a pause, "You're the cop off the internet,"

"I can smell alcohol off your breath, and your eyes suggest the recent use of an A-class substance," said Crowe, catching his breath,

"You nearly killed a man," said Fionn,

"Trust me, pal, I'm only just warming up," said Crowe.

Fionn rose and dusted off the sand. His face was peppered with it. He somehow reassembled his hard-man look and leapt onto the slipway.

"I had nothing to do with it. Nothing, d'you hear? We weren't the only ones, loser fool Hunt. That's who should be fucking talkin…" he said gasping, "… held us up looking for his lucky charm, had us going around in circles. He was crying as much…"

Hunt. Mr photophobia sunglasses and Lear jet Cheltenham jaunts, thought Crowe.

Then Fionn slapped his hand over his mouth like kid who had spoken out of turn in class. Wide-eyed, he paced a few more times up and down the slipway, stumbling. Crowe edged backwards toward the relative safety of the car park, mindful of the slippery moss under his feet.

Fionn leapt into the Merc. The engine ground to life and the vehicle lurched forward. Crowe side-stepped deftly back onto the car park. The huge engine turned over once, then growled into life. With the smell of burning tyres, the SUV and trailer swung off the slipway and accelerated into the town.

In Crowe's mind he saw Quigley holding a snifter of brandy. After a hefty swig, he twisted the crystal stopper into the decanter.

"Thought I'd stir the pot, just like old times, Quigley," murmured Crowe.

"To old times, P.J."

Quigley. Where the hell was he?

A Kind of Drowning

<u>24</u>

"You've started a shit-storm, Crowe," said Thea.

Crowe could smell the salt-tang of burning driftwood from beneath a large steel drum. They were on the beach of the small cove on Inishcarrig, the spit was long and winding into the turbulent sea. It was early evening and it was getting cold. Crowe could hear the crying gulls.

"Run then, Mr. Grumpy," she said, it was Thea, but somehow even more so. Her eyes had sunken into her skull, the skin tight and yellow, her hair was lank and unkempt. It was missing in places around her waxen skull.

The breeze was picking up. Thea looked up,

"He's coming," she said.

Sounds of laughter came from behind. Crowe turned; Alison was there, in her jeans and heavy jumper. She was wearing her hair up. Unable to move, rooted to the spot, Crowe watched helplessly as Alison turned and started walking along the spit,

"Give Cathal a kiss for me," he shouted.

Alison ignored him and started walking out to sea along the spit…

Crowe woke up in a sweat. Checking his phone the time read 11:00am. No messages returned by Quigley. Crowe dialled but was only going straight to voicemail.

Where the fuck was the fat chungus bastard?

Opening the curtains, he studied the pall of cloud that belched intense pulses of rain across Roscarrig. Through the glass, the roofs of the town resembled a smeared charcoal sketch. The courtyard below was shiny with exploding droplets. A gutter opposite was a waterfall, drumming onto the bins. There was no sign of the fox, come to think of it, he hadn't seen it in a few days. He surveyed the room; a stack of lager cans lay strewn around a three-quarter empty bottle of Jameson

A Kind of Drowning

which had toppled over. A crumpled fish and chip supper bag stood sentinel at the table's edge. After doing several fruitless circuits and smarting from the dinner from hell, he had eventually found the main street and stumbled upon a chip shop about to close up for the night.

Opening out the window, Crowe tossed out the greasy paper bag and watched its buffeted descent more out of hope than anything else. It sycamored gracefully, landing between the bins.

"Come and get it, fox" he whispered as he wrestled the window shut.

The damp yellow tee stretched across his gut. He found amid the cans, an unfinished shot glass of whiskey shining like an amber jewel. He swilled and downed it in a gulp. Scratching himself idly, he opened a new pack of cigarettes. The nicotine hit his synapses like a freight train. He put the kettle on and pulled on a fleece and reasonably clean sweat pants. As he stowed away the bed and bundled the bedding, he heard the bang of the outer door.

His phone beeped a message from Derry – *TROUBLE ON THE WAY NOW!*

What the fuck was Gallagher going on about?

Through the funk of an hangover, he thought that maybe Gallagher was planning to evict him;. Crowe eyed the defunct smoke alarm guiltily.

He looked around his living room. He took down the case board and slid it under the sofa bed. He tidied up the table and put the pens, post-its and A4 pads in a cupboard. As a precaution he slotted his phone in his pocket with the voice recorder activated.

The coke.

A Kind of Drowning

He walked into the bathroom and with a few folded sheets of toilet paper, he reached under the S-bend and retrieved it. He stuffed his hands into the pockets of the hoodie.

He heard Gallagher's booming voice rising through the three flights of stairwell. As an early warning system, Gallagher had his uses. Crowe steeled himself. He positioned himself as far away from the front door as possible, pressing his back against the kitchen wall.

He heard the key in the garret's lock rattle and turn and the door opened.

In walked Gallagher followed by Teflon D, cap pulled low and chomping on gum like a twelve year old.

"Nice company you're keeping these days, Derry," said Crowe.

"You've been asking after me, hassling my kid and generally disturbing the peace, so I thought I'd pop around and introduce myself, formally - I'm Desmond,"

Teflon held out a hand, the thumb was missing. Teflon D himself in the flesh.

"I know who you are," said Crowe.

"Don't leave me hanging?" said Teflon D. His hand remained extended. Crowe folded his arms.

"We've met already," said Crowe,

"Don't remember it, sport,"

"Roman coins, Vikings and moving contraband. Seems your son, Fionn has taken up your interest in local archaeology? As I always say, a man should have a hobby. Meant to ask that day, what happened there, Des?"

A Kind of Drowning

Crowe nodded to the missing digit.

Teflon D with his other thumb pushed the baseball cap high on his head and gave a rueful smile,

"This? Oh, Lost that thumb here to a Chinaman. You see, I had notions, yes, ideas about myself and my place in the world. Told a Chink to fuck off over an unpaid debt and lost a thumb for my troubles. They tossed it in the canal right in front of me. They left me by the canal bank. Broken nose, two teeth on the ground and a missing thumb. I had to walk two miles to a hospital as they'd taken my wallet. Rookie mistake, I was only a chisler then. A salutary lesson, sport. A salutary lesson. One you are about to learn, sport," said Teflon D.

His smile was pulled taut around his skull. Crowe took in Teflon, built like a spinning top and giving off kingpin waves like a full-power microwave oven. He smelled of shower gel and chewing gum. Underneath the Northface jacket, body armour creaked. Kevlar, the urban criminal's badge of honour.   "So gents, what's the story?" said Crowe.

"Desmond here wanted to have a chat with you," said Gallagher.

Sweat was beading around Gallagher's face, his carefully woven hair was coming loose. He looked terrified.

"Well, here I am," said Crowe. His levelled gaze at Teflon said, *you're nothing but shit on the shoe…*

Teflon raised his hand up toward Gallagher in a genial karate chop. Gallagher flinched like a beaten dog. Teflon D leered,

"Your friend Derry here, smells like a tart's handkerchief, doesn't he? All hand cream, aftershave, and hairspray. Not like us working men, you, and me. I've always hated the smell of eau de toilette. Spent a summer on the killing floor in a slaughterhouse in

Perth; blood, piss, shit, dead meat, and the girls on the packing lines sweating out their deodorants, well, those that bothered. One hell of a stench, Crowe isn't it? Garda Inspector Pius John Crowe? I'll get to the point; I think you're in the wrong town, sport,"

"You think so?" replied Crowe.

"Know so," said Teflon D, "I think you need to find a new one."

"New one?" said Crowe, refusing to be baited.

His grip around the twist of coke tightened. He kept both hands in his hoodie.

"I'll be brief. I hear you've been sniffing around; asking questions, making general enquiries and being an all-round, fucking pain in the arse. So I start asking around myself and lo and behold, I discover the old pig, Quigley has a new tenant. Another copper, a pig. Imagine that? Then I hear he's the YouTube sensation, Pius John Crowe. AKA 'PODGE'. Hashtag *MadGardaBastard*. One step from a suicide, I hear. A burn-out, a fuck-up and a mental case to boot – is that true?" grinned Teflon D.

Crowe remained silent and stared.

"Then I'm asking my ol' segotia, Derry here; he and Quigley go back a ways, funny money and bouncing cheques, so the story goes. And I ask him: Where. The. Fuck. Is the burn-out? And now here we are. SO, pig, you need to find a new location. The last thing I need is some basket case hobbling around my town. Or making a nuisance of himself on my island. It is what it is,"

"I thought Quigley had warned you, your days are numbered?" said Crowe.

"I told him, I said 'you're retired and riddled with cancer, Quigley - why don't you fuck off somewhere with a fishing rod and enjoy whatever time is left? Get right with your God, sport' Maybe that's what he's done. Gone fishin',"

Cancer, thought Crowe, how would a scumbag like Teflon know?

"Unlike Quigley, I doubt you'll be around long enough to see the old age pension, *Teflon*," replied Crowe.

This raised a nervous titter from Gallagher.

"A warning from a burned-out pig and another one from a pig that's dying - now I'm intrigued," murmured Teflon D.

"I'm not leaving Roscarrig until I find out what happened to the girl," said Crowe. Time to wrong foot this goon before he starts waxing lyrical again.

"What girl?" replied Teflon D.

"The girl who drowned, Thea." said Crowe.

"The dummy? The slow person, the special needs kid? No loss, the world is better off without it,"

Crowe's sudden flash of anger spurred Teflon on,

"Collateral damage, former Garda Inspector Pius John Crowe. As I always say, the devil is in the detail the - Ts and Cs. If they're too fucking slow to understand I can't accept any responsibility,"

Crowe watched Teflon take a step closer. Menace flowed from every pore.

Come on, thought Crowe. *Get a little closer, fuckwit.* How much battery life was left on the phone? The two men's shoes squeaked, and the floorboards groaned as the space between them tightened.

A Kind of Drowning

"Her name was Thea," said Crowe, "T-H-E-A,"

"Why are you speaking slowly?" asked Teflon.

"Because I'm not sure you understand basic English, *Sport*. You look a bit fucking special yourself," said Crowe.

Crowe was ready for the punch. He rolled his head with it. Teflon grunted with the exertion. The vest must have inhibited his swing, but the explosion across Crowe's jaw did enough to cause some bleeding to the gums.

"Gentlemen, please!" shouted Gallagher.

"Get your fucking hands up, you cunt," hissed Teflon D.

Crowe just grinned. Their eyes locked. Then Teflon D produced a pistol. He brandished it around Crowe's face like a conjuror pulling a bazooka out of a hat.

A Walther P99. Fuck.

"Threatening a member of the public with a firearm? In front of a witness?" said Crowe.

"Derry here, knows the score. He'll keep shtum. As I said, moron, you're in the wrong town. You have until midnight to get off my patch,"

"Or?"

"I'll pay another visit. Put a bullet in your spine and fuck you up like a road accident. After that, I'll find that son of yours, Cathal isn't it? Kid crying on YouTube? Did me a little search before we arrived. He'd be easy to find and I'll put a bullet in his skull. Fuck him up too," grinned Teflon D.

Crowe's head butt was so fast, Gallagher thought he had been seeing things. The clash of skulls sounded like a wrecking ball swinging between a pair of rhinos. The gun clattered to the floor and Crowe wrangled enough space to lock Teflon D in a head lock and deliver two hefty blows into the side of the neckless skull.

"I'll think about it," said Crowe.

Gallagher got himself between them.

"Jesus, lads, stop."

His voice was shrill.

"STOP."

The three wrenched themselves free. Crowe kicked the pistol away towards the door. Teflon straightened up and swung. Crowe dodged it but collided with the table. Teflon clawed air. Gallagher dived back in between them. He turned and tried to herd Teflon toward the door.

"I've business to attend to today. I want you out by midnight. Off my turf do you understand, pig? Off my turf," Teflon spat at Crowe.

"I'm staying. I like it here, taking the air is conducive for my recuperation," said Crowe, he tugged his hoodie back into shape and ran his tongue around his gums. A little blood, but nothing loose.

"No one will mourn a burn-out like you. I'd be doing your bosses a favour putting you out of your misery. Time to get right with your God, dickwad."

Teflon picked up the gun and slid it under the jacket.

"let's go Gallagher,"

"Where are you off to lads? Anywhere nice? Can I come along?" said Crowe.

"Fuck off, Looney Tunes," said Teflon D.

A Kind of Drowning

"In your car, Derry? Hope you're not up to any shenanigans with Thumbelina there?" said Crowe.

Gallagher made pleading eyes through his glasses, then turned on his heel.

Teflon turned and glowered as Gallagher cajoled him out. He made a shooting gesture with his left hand.

Crowe was shaken. He lit a cigarette and poured another whiskey, emptying the last of the bottle. He rinsed the alcohol around his mouth and spat into the sink. A few rivulets of blood, but nothing serious. So, Thumbelina threatened to shoot Cathal, a man who would threaten a child would hurt one too under the right conditions.

To hurt a woman wouldn't be a leap. A young woman like Thea.

The twist of cocaine, that little inconvenient hit was now wedged securely in Teflon D's windcheater.

Crowe reached for his mobile and stopped the recorder. He played the recording back, it was indistinct in places, but Teflon-one-thumb's voice was clear. Pity no-one had shouted 'GUN!' He sent the audio as an attachment to Liv Cutts.

Then he dialled 999, as any concerned citizen would do if they suspected a crime. He gave his name, former rank, and badge number. Derry's car registration was easy to remember, and for good measure, Crowe added the make and colour. Maybe THE BIG MACHINE was ready to forgive.

Every little helps, he thought. He had to be somewhere himself.

In the bathroom, he checked his face for any bruising. His left eye was still smarting from Teflon's headbutt. All he could see in his left side vision was a deep red with a cosmos of dancing yellow dots. His jaw on that side radiated pain. It felt swollen. That said looking at the reflection, outwardly, he thought he'd pass muster. Then Crowe shaved, working the razor gingerly around the sore points and as he towelled his face, went to the kitchen to boil the kettle for a coffee. He made a cup of instant, lit a cigarette and scanned around the room to see if anything would make a good parcel.

Then he donned his heavy black fleece, tugged on the hi-viz vest, and pulled his baseball cap down low over his eyebrows.

***

The old vicarage Aoife had mentioned in the restaurant wasn't hard to find. Crowe must have passed it dozens of times on his walks, but it's obscurity and foliage had made it inconspicuous. It was situated in off the coast road, with a spectacular rolling view of Inishcarrig. The high wall and the house's grand façade was made of old stone peppered with ancient dark green ivy. A bank of security cameras along the guttering and a modern-looking keypad inset at the high gate told Crowe all he needed to know. In his hand he had a library book stuffed into a chip bag and sellotaped up. There'd be hell to pay with Clodagh about the grease stains, but that would be later.

He pressed the intercom buzzer, a crackling 'yes?' came through. He held the package up at the small camera,

"I've a delivery for Mr. Hunt?" said Crowe.

There was a pause,

"Registered post – for Hunt?"

The gates whirred open and he walked up the crescent-shaped pebble driveway framed by neatly tended beds. He looked at the heavy duty lawn roller propped against the ride-on mower and side-stepped past the freshly planted saplings, bound and staked to the earth. Crowe wandered around to the back of the building.

A Kind of Drowning

There he found two jet-skis mounted on a trailer.

Without breaking stride, he photographed them with his phone and made his way to the front door. For once he had a strong signal and sent the images to Cutts' mobile. He remembered when freshly minted out of Templemore, he had walked the beat with Quigley,

"How do you find a crime?" he'd asked.

"Simple, son," Quigley replied, *"You fall over it,"*

Crowe rang the ornate doorbell and waited patiently to see who would open the door.

25

Ephraim Hunt didn't do quieter moments. Quieter moments meant something was happening elsewhere outside of his ken. It was his mind tossing ideas around like a monkey house on Red Bull, that had made him the success he was – or had been. It was all about mindset. Beside his expensive espresso machine, his replacement iPhone pulsed to the beat of the modern-day Netizen. The wall mounted flatscreen was showing a news report; people in facemasks confronting lines of riot police who were firing tear gas into them. This Avian Flu seemed to be popping up everywhere, stealthily appearing on all the social media feeds. The markets were getting jittery; the Nikkei and Hang Sen were looking like disaster zones right now. Dow Jones and FTSE just as unstable.

His view of Dublin was marred by the rain, meddling with his buzz. The Samuel Beckett Bridge, pristine, strung and white, guided his eyes along the grey river Liffey as it snaked back towards the Four Courts. His gaze then continued out to the high rises of Kilmainham and further out to the distant gang turfs of Crumlin and Tallaght where he'd dragged himself into rough respectability.

Lean and toned from a ruthless regime of squats, five-a-side football, and charity half-marathons, he skated across the kitchen. Along the corridor of his penthouse, framed pictures of his wild-card successes hung on one side like the platinum and gold discs of a 1970's Billboard Top 100. On the opposite wall, he posed with the various MMA warrior gods caught in the camera flash, with his default *'What? Who me?'* expression for the camera. The local boy done good pose. He was the comeback kid, Mr. Fleetwood Mac. In five hours, Hunt and his legal team would wrench a decade of confiscated tenders and plans out of the bear-trap of NAMA. Then the party would begin big-time. He had champagne cooling in the vast fridge, a new box of Lonsdale's ready to be broken out and a crème-de-la-crème pouch of Columbian pure white gold ready for the celebration.

Hunt changed into his running gear, then preened in front of the full length mirror and finally checked his nostrils. Bouncing out into the lobby, he pressed for the elevator to the underground car park. The sunlight burned through the sunglasses, searing his retinas. He worried a hangnail with his teeth and felt the time lag through the elevator's slow descent.

He wasn't expecting the burly man with a face like a butcher's dog.

If he could have hit the shut button he would have, only Crowe was already in the elevator. Crowe pressed the Close Door button without breaking eye contact.

"Who the fuck are you?" asked Hunt, reaching for the emergency alarm button.

"I've a few questions, Hunt," said Crowe, gripping Hunt's hand and wrenched it back on the wrist, twisting it away from the control panel.

"Contact my people, get out of my face" said Hunt pulling his hand free.

"I know what you did on Inishcarrig." said Crowe.

"What are you taking about?" replied Hunt evasively.

He tried to push past Crowe.

Crowe slammed him up against the wall.

"I know you were out there with the Cosgrave gang. I want to find out what happened to Thea Farrell."

It was a crude gambit. He wasn't in the mood to deal in any clever verbal jousting. He smacked Hunt open-handed across the face,

"I had nothing to do with, I swear," said Hunt.

A Kind of Drowning

"You've seen one of these before," said Crowe. He flashed his badge in front of Hunt. It was the one thing he had kept all this time. The one thing he wouldn't hand over to Internal Affairs, claiming that during his breakdown, he had tossed it into the Liffey. To remove this badge would have erased his identity.

"This is my national police credential, Ephraim Hunt. Thea Farrell. I believe she was the victim of a crime. It is my belief you were involved in that said crime,"

He pressed the metal badge into the side of Hunt's face.

"I'm telling you; you're talking to the wrong fella. It was those…animals…the twins," stammered Hunt.

"And you,"

"No," gasped Hunt.

Crowe put the badge wallet away and held up his phone in front of Hunt,

"I saw you land and take off from the island of Inishcarrig. I requested this information as part of an ongoing Garda investigation, it tallies with my sighting of you. This is a screenshot of your helicopter's flight plan submitted to the IAA. On the plan there's another passenger; Casey Clarke. Bet she'd love to know her boyfriend attacked a special needs girl with a bunch of thugs. Would love to see what a stand-up kind of guy you are, with all your charity stuff 'n all. I've evidence linking the island to drug smuggling and your involvement in it. And your connection to a criminal known to the gardai, living, and operating in Roscarrig just down the road from your second home in the town. Coincidence? I don't believe in them. Catch my drift?"

Hunt's prominent Adam's apple danced up and down. The tinted lenses skewed from the slap magnified his disjointed terror. He started gulping for air, and the tears began to pinch at his eyes,

"How did you find me anyway?" he asked.

Crowe slapped him again. This time harder.

"Your Facebook page, sir," said Crowe, "…and your housekeeper, a Ms. Gosia Sankiewicz at your residence, The Church House, in Roscarrig was very helpful with my enquiries. She informed me that you're supposed to be on the Six-One News tonight. The Business This Week feature?"

"Yes and I'm going to be late, Garda…?"

"I'd make alternate arrangements, Hunt," said Crowe.

He scrolled to the next photo and held it up.

"Two jet skis. In your back garden. I saw an identical one being hitched to Fionn Cosgrave's vehicle. He practically threw you under the bus. I barely had to nudge him,"

Hunt's mercurial mind had slammed on the brakes. His mouth began to make fish movements.

"Nothing you have said proves anything," he said.

"I found something on the island. A cigar tube, and guess what was in it?" said Crowe.

Hunt's expression loosened as if every bolt holding it had unwound a turn.

"Yep, a US Dollar bill," said Crowe.

He let the sentence hang.

"Granules of grade A cocaine. So my prints will be eliminated by the Crime technicians, which leaves…?" he gave Hunt a shove as a prompt. "Yours, I'll wager,"

A Kind of Drowning

Hunt's glasses tumbled off his nose. In the harsh metallic light, his skin was waxen and dark circles hung about his eyes. A life of excess was etched into his taut features,

"Yes, probably," he whispered.

"Bet your prints are on Thea's Nike too, its already at the crime lab,"

Hunt clenched his eyes shut, dropped his shoulders, and in the confined space, seemed to fold into himself. He remembered the shadows of the night. On the island with the three Teflon boys. The feral laughs of the pumped-up twins Fionn and Setanta.

"Giveitback, giveitbacktome, please…please",

"That fucking shoe," murmured Hunt, "I told them not to. They made a game of it - Piggy-in-the-middle. I told them to hand it back and stop taking the piss. They were playing rough. Too rough. All I remember is at the end there was a long scream. I have tried really fucking hard to forget that sound,"

As Hunt struggled to push the memory back into the furthest recesses of his mind. He began to sob.

The shrill wail that Hunt emitted jackhammered into Crowe's prefrontal cortex. He was aching and tired; he needed to pop some Ibuprofen.

"Who?" asked Crowe, "who was playing rough?"

"The Cosgrave twins, Fionn and Setanata, they were making the hog sounds – you know, teasing her like, tossing her shoe?" said Hunt. Merely speaking unlocked his memory,

He reached deeper into the moments, trying to piece together what happened next. But it came up blank,

A Kind of Drowning

"I was in pain you see? We had everything in place - The deal was *'done'*. Norcott's team was prepared to hand the island over. A cool one-hundred million revenue stream ready to be tapped into," said Hunt.

"Then Desmond Cosgrave got wind of it?" said Crowe.

Hunt was sweating, his rank terror was filling up the narrow confines of the elevator space.

"They kidnapped me, threw me onto their boat and did this!" he said holding up a bandaged finger, "Cut the tip off with a chisel, a fucking wood chisel,"

The boat, a luxury forty foot, had slowed gradually, bumping along the swells towards an aged stone jetty.

"Now, you're going to give me a guided tour of your island. Your Driftwood Golf Resort, yeah?" said Teflon D, "Silent partner, sport, yeah?"

Hunt had been in agony, cold and terrified. They had beaten him again on the journey back. Then threw him into the boot of their cat. Outside the penthouse, they tossed him out onto the pavement, before screeching out into the dawn. He had shut his mind down to that night, drawn a long black curtain across his memory. Staring at his patched-up finger, he noticed his hand had begun to shake uncontrollably.

Wracking with sobs, Hunt blurted, "On the way back in Teflon D's boat I drank myself stupid, trying to numb the pain. Champagne, brandy, half a bottle of Powers. They threatened to hurt Casey. Rape her," the Cosgraves' laughter had come back in flashbacks through the last few days.

He didn't even remember getting into bed.

Crowe fought every urge to start punching Hunt.

"Like I said, you're a solid, stand-up guy, Hunt," he said.

"They slung her," said Hunt.

"What?" said Crowe.

"What's her name, the piggy-in-the-middle. The retard," said Hunt.

Crowe hoisted Hunt up off his feet, pressing him hard against the cold steel wall of the elevator.

"Thea Farrell was dredged up from the fucking sea," yelled Crowe.

Struggling, Hunt turned away from Crowe's glare, the twitching facial muscles and the bellowing mouth millimetres from his face. Then Crowe released Hunt. Crowe jabbed the Open Door button and the doors whispered open. He gave one glance back at the man crumpled and sobbing on the floor of an elevator in a luxury apartment complex, with a mixture of pity and loathing.

He walked back through the underground carpark towards the main street. Once he got a signal, he dialled 999. The rain was still teeming down, and people dashed through the puddles towards Connolly Railway Station. LUAS trams rumbled and hissed along their sleepers. Crowe buried himself deeper into his faded damp fleece waiting. The rain was unforgiving, and rivulets ran through his clothing. After a few minutes, a patrol car pulled in and two Gardai emerged festooned with the paraphernalia of leads and wires that led to ear pieces and two-way radios.

"Ephraim Hunt," said Crowe displaying his badge, "I left him in the elevator. He's all yours."

As the police walked toward the complex an unmarked squad car pulled up. O'Suilleabháin leaned out of the passenger side. He stared at Crowe,

"Voice recorder might not be admissible," admitted Crowe. He handed his phone over to O'Suilleabháin.

"You didn't try anything stupid like a citizen's arrest did you?" asked O'Suilleabháin.

"No. I'm going home now," replied Crowe.

O'Suilleabháin turned the phone over in his hands, "This phone looks like you, Crowe, a heap o' shite. I'll hand it over to the tekkies. We have a forensics crew on the island looking for your girl's Nike. Let's hope for your sake, they find something. Want a lift anywhere?"

"Her name was Thea. And no, I don't need a lift," replied Crowe, tapping out a cigarette. He sparked it up.

Chief Superintendent Dáithí O'Suilleabháin regarded Crowe standing dishevelled in the rain with something close to pity,

"We got Cosgrave. Teflon is cooling his heels in Store Street Garda Station. But remember, the likes of him and Hunt get the very best legal,"

"Buy cheap, you get cheap," said Crowe, "those K-Pop twins of his?"

"Gone. Got a 4.30am flight to Malaga yesterday. The Notorious Dubs have fucked off to see their mammy in Spain."

"Blistering reaction times as usual," said Crowe.

He turned away and set off for the railway station before O'Suilleabháin could get the last word in.

On the North bound inter-city out of Connolly, Crowe dozed in the empty carriage until it pulled into Roscarrig station. Checking his wrist, he remembered he didn't have a watch. Patting his damp fleece, he remembered he no longer had a phone.

26

August

Crowe stared out at the sea. Inishcarrig was shrouded in a heavy mist. It was cold. Leaden clouds clung low to the horizon. Crowe pulled his woollen hat down and shrugged deeper into his fleece. Clodagh linked his arm and sidled in closer.

"So, are you sticking around?" she asked.

Derry Gallagher, fresh from his brush with the law, had extended the garret's lease. The summer season had collapsed after the flu outbreak and if it were possible, Roscarrig had slipped further into morbid decline.

"The lease is until the end of the year, so yes, I might," replied Crowe.

She prised another chip out of Crowe's take-away bag spread out across his lap. The weather-beaten bench they were sitting on was flanked by a JCB standing idle. The town council had marked out an area to build a memorial to Thea. Local schoolkids had collected rocks along the strand and painted them in a rainbow of colours. They were scattered around the edge of the site.

"I'm not sure what will happen in the new year," he said.

Quigley was dead. It had come as a shock to Crowe. Admitted with respiratory problems as a result of the Asian Flu, Quigley lingered for forty-eight hours before succumbing. Stage four cancer had eroded his capacity to fight the illness. He had died alone in an empty ICU hooked up to a ventilator. He had no next of kin. The Garda Press Office had distributed this notification internally. Liv Cutts had forwarded it to Crowe's private Gmail. No-one to attend any services as a result of the emergency situation. No flowers, only cash donations to The Irish Cancer Society.

A Kind of Drowning

Crowe tapped out another B&H and lit it. The breeze whipped the smoke skywards.

"You know secondary smoke does just as much damage?" she said.

"You enjoy the odd drag," he replied.

"Only when I was drinking," she said.

"You were more fun then," he said.

"Can you please blow it in the other direction, Crowe?"

"Helps me think," replied Crowe.

She waved the cigarette smoke away,

"You can think elsewhere, Crowe – put that thing out,"

They saw Ned's vessel ploughing the waves. The sea looked grey and treacherous,

"Were you out in that?" asked Crowe.

"This morning? Yes, it was exhilarating," she said

"That's one word for it," replied Crowe.

"Baby steps on the road to recovery," she said, "I've been sober for a month,"

"I thought it was just a phase," said Crowe.

He stubbed out the cigarette on the iron armrest. The sparks and ashes were snatched by the breeze.

"What time is your meeting tomorrow?" she asked

"Ten," replied Crowe.

A Kind of Drowning

He dug out the last crispy shards of chips and proffered them. Clodagh picked at a few and Crowe tossed the remainder down his throat. He gave a low long belch.

"Still know how to show a girl a good time," she said.

"It's how I roll," he replied.

Crowe scrunched up the takeaway bag into a tight ball and lobbed it towards the bin. It glanced off the top and ricocheted wildly into the grass. With a sigh, he dusted off the crumbs and ambled over to the bag. A seagull strutted a few feet away from him eyeing the bag's progress as the breeze caught and tumbled it.

Crowe binned the greasy bag and looked back. Clodagh had forgiven him for the dinner fiasco. As a form of apology, he cooked a spaghetti and invited her over for dinner. He hadn't spilled or knocked anything over, so to him that was a result. And like Cinderella she had fled the garret before midnight. Since then, they seemed to have moved into a gradual parallel orbit. Yet something unresolved, something uncertain remained. They hadn't moved on to sleeping together; Crowe sensed Clodagh was wrestling with an internal conflict. He didn't want to push anything that could get wildly out of control.

They were happy with the uncomplicated companionship for now.

But nothing was ever uncomplicated.

He crooked an elbow. With a smile, Clodagh got up, linked his arm and they walked along.

"Thanks for lunch, even if it was out of a bag," she said.

"My pleasure," he replied.

For the past few weeks, he had noticed she was clear of eye and not masking the undertow of booze with gum. He admired her determination; he wasn't brave enough yet.

They stopped to look at the mist clearing from the island, sending the temperature down. They walked in silence to the library. As she opened it up for the afternoon, Crowe said,

"Clodagh,"

She turned and looked at him.

"Alison and I have formally separated," said Crowe.

"I see," said Clodagh, "Well, as we're going for full disclosure, I got you a little something,"

"Hardly worth celebrating,"

"Our timing is as impeccable as always," she said.

From her bag she produced a small, gift-wrapped package. Crowe opened it out. Inside the wrapping was a fridge magnet. It was a pen and ink image of the Boogie-Woogie Café's facade with a bold pink **'Don't worry, be happy'.**

"You might want to actually put things in the fridge, so this should remind you," she said.

Crowe leaned in and kissed her on the cheek. The bristles of his beard brushed gently against her skin,

"Have a good afternoon, and please, please, please keep torturing the old biddies," he said.

"It's what I do best," she replied.

Crowe stuffed his hands into his jacket and walked. He walked past the Library, cutting across the carpark. Past the garage where the man behind the counter wore a surgical mask. Past the supermarket with the hanging flower pots and, avoiding the ankle-wrenching dip just outside Gallagher Estates. A sign in the door read 'Closed for Lunch', and Crowe smiled at the thought of Derry Gallagher regaling his fans at the

A Kind of Drowning

Boogie-Woogie Café again about how he had brought down an underworld Kingpin.

The rain began to pummel down making his running shoes damp. He opened the door to the stairwell beside The Dragon Inn. He tramped up the staircase and turned his key in the lock. The cramped apartment had gradually absorbed his presence. He filled the kettle and reached for a jar of instant coffee. The smells from the Chinese and the cawing of hungry gulls made him close up the skylight and windows.

Crowe made an instant coffee and placing it on the table, reached into the shiny new suit carrier that was hanging up at the door. He took down the suit, removing the tags and opened out the shirt. Clodagh had helped him pick out both.

Crowe tried it on with the shoes.

They pinched at the little toe and cut into the heel.

But it would do.

In the corner of the room he had a black bin liner filled with his old clothes. Probably fit for an incinerator, a fleece, some Ts and his frayed cargo pants spilled out like an exotic potted plant. On the floor was a crumpled business card. He picked it up. Before tossing it into the bin, he turned it over. The text was faded from water, but the thin white cross and Abosede's taxi contact number were clear,

Crowe smiled,

He dialled the number,

    "Can I order a taxi for tomorrow? Roscarrig to Dublin City. 8am. My mobile is…"

He showered, shaved, and spent the evening trawling through Netflix without settling on a programme. The Dragon Inn's menu had expanded its repertoire to Thai cuisine and for the first time since April, he didn't down a few cans as an accompaniment.

Green tea was the devil's piss he thought as he sipped it.

His phone chirruped a notification; *A statement from An Taoiseach live from Government Buildings: "After consultation with the HSE and the NPHET, it has been decided that a Phase One Lockdown will commence with immediate effect from tomorrow at midnight,"*

Christ, he thought.

He didn't sleep that night.

27

It was Crowe's kind of ride, neither he nor Abosede spoke. The windscreen wipers fought with what sounded like a month of rainfall drumming on the roof. The adhesive 3-D Jesus stared back at him, frozen in absolvement. The thick-beaded wooden rosary swung lazily from the mirror at every turn. Abosede was resplendent in green.

He remembered what she had said as he arrived in Roscarrig; *"Believe in the Lord Jesus and you will be saved,"*

Hadn't Jesus walked on water? thought Crowe. Though if he had spent a summer in Roscarrig, Christ might have failed the challenge.

It wasn't until the lines of greenhouses amid large tracts of grass and ragwort were in the rear view mirrors that Abosede spoke,

"I remember you now, the blessed stranger in that nowhere town," she said, "You pay good. Pay like a top boss man,"

Her voice was rich and deep. She spoke with absolute assurance.

"I'm flattered," he replied.

She turned her flawless profile,

"You still look done in, man. Good suit though."

"I'll take that as a compliment," he replied.

"You police?" she asked.

"I'll know later today,"

Abosede grinned "Ah! I knew you were police. Crowe. The man all over the news."

It sounded like *"Crouwe."*

"Pius John Crowe, the same," he replied.

"Old news now," she said.

The cab smelled exotic. The AC was set to tropical. He remembered the gold watch. It glowed on her ebony skin; the crystal was still cracked, and the face had gold numerals. He looked at his wrist, he needed to get a watch.

He needed to smoke,

"May I?" he asked producing a packet of B&H.

Abosede tapped a gloriously painted nail at the no smoking sign.

The motorway appeared. The rain had finally stopped, and the thunderheads rolled south.

"There were checkpoints in Dublin this morning, man. Terrible," said Abosede.

"I hear there's a lockdown coming," said Crowe.

"You lucky I could collect you. People afraid to go out. LUAS, DART stopped – only buses running Sunday timetables. Pity 'cos the city is money, now no money. Now no city,"

She turned on the radio. Crowe watched the stations scroll on the dashboard,

"… and that was 'DoubleFace' by the Notorious Dubs Setanta and Fionn, aka NDSF. Check out their latest Instagram story on life in Spain…" trilled the DJ on an entertainment station.

"Anything else? A news station please?" said Crowe.

Humming 'DoubleFace', Abosede settled on a local news station. The programme faded in and out on the bandwidth. The white lines of the motorway flowed before them. There were few cars. Morning rush hour and hardly a vehicle. Abosede floored the accelerator.

A Kind of Drowning

Avian Flu crisis was the headline. With infection rates climbing, people were requested to work from home. Avoid all unnecessary travel. The newscaster was in the middle of an interview with a spokesman for civil rights. The line was poor, but the strident tone of the spokesman cut through it. An excuse for a Garda clampdown on ordinary citizens was the main concern.

"Any station playing classical?" asked Crowe.

With a sigh, Abosede searched for a light classical station. Debussy drifted around the cab.

"The end is nigh, you mark my words," said Abosede.

"That's a cheery thought. Am I right, your brother is a preacher?" said Crowe

"That is correct, he have a church on Dawson Street," replied Abosede.

"Business must be good?"

"Very. Very good. He preaches twice every day. You're welcome anytime,"

Crowe was about to respond when she decelerated suddenly. A Garda checkpoint appeared closing off all the lanes. A tall guard wearing a black face mask guided them into a siding on the hard shoulder.

He walked toward the taxi. Crowe knew the type. Hard. Kitted out for a riot.

Abosede rolled down the window.

"This man must get to Dublin, Guard. Very urgent."

The Guard looked at them both. His eyes were cold and penetrating above the mask.

Crowe released his seat belt and reached into the suit. He pulled out the letter and handed it to Abosede. She practically shoved it into the Guard's face.

He read it. Droplets of rain water fell off the peaked cap. He handed the letter back to her,

"Thank you, Guard," she said.

He acknowledged her with the barest of nods and looked in at Crowe, pulling his mask down.

"Good luck, Crowe. You'll need it," he said.

Abosede started up the engine and revved out through the road block. The taxi hurtled through the Dublin Port Tunnel coming out along the docks. At the roundabout at The East Link, she turned right, and Crowe began to feel the first twinges of unease. She pulled in sharply at the IFSC Quayside Quarter and snapped on the hazards,

"Want me to wait?" she asked

Crowe looked at the meter. He handed her two fifties.

"No. Thank you, but no. I don't know how long I'll be in there. Keep the change,"

"I'll see you around, Mr. Crowe," she said.

"I'll see you around, Abosede. Don't go back the way you came. That check point clocked you doing 140 in an 120 zone. Don't give them an excuse,"

Crowe stepped out of the cab and straightened his suit. Abosede launched her cab like a Formula One race car out of the pitstop. Her brake lights flashed a couple of times and then she was gone.

A Kind of Drowning

Harris the union rep was waiting for Crowe on the steps of the HR Offices. Dublin's pavements were a sheen of puddles reflecting the early morning sun.

"You're looking well, Podge," said Harris.

The collar of Crowe's shirt was too tight and its slim-fit cut somehow managed to exaggerate his gut. He left the top button open and the jacket fastened. *'Stylishly dressed down'* Clodagh called it

"Living by the seaside helps, Harris," replied Crowe.

Harris nodded. Staring up at the sky, he pursed his lips which made it seem as though his face was collapsing. Cupped in his fist was a crudely made roll-up. His suit had seen better days, thrown on as an afterthought.

"Lucky bastard," he said.

From his leather zip folder, he handed Crowe a padded envelope. Crowe opened it. Inside was his old phone, the top rust-coloured in dried blood.

"There was a watch with it? A Citizen, black leather strap?"

"Good luck with that," grinned Harris.

Crowe put the phone in his inside pocket, then crumpled up the padded envelope.

"Hear there's a lockdown?" he asked.

"Only announced last night, but the department's been on a crisis footing for a fortnight now. My eyes are cunten square with ZOOM meetings. Excruciating man. Miss the road, getting out of this city."

Lowering his voice, tilting his mouth up at one corner Harris scanned the passers-by over the rim of his round framed glasses. Sometimes he was known as Lennon or Himmler, depending on who you spoke to.

"That little hit of coke I slipped you, did it help?" he asked.

"It did," replied Crowe,

"You looked like you needed it," said Harris.

He rubbed his nose as a reflex.

"Who will it be this morning?" asked Crowe

"Townsend and O'Suilleabháin," replied Harris.

"Fuck," muttered Crowe.

"Fuck indeed, Podge. She's the Minister's golden girl; Justice Minister Gartland's attack dog, using the emergency to go after some of our members,"

"Some of us deserve it," said Crowe.

Harris pinched off the tip of the roll-up, extinguishing the ash, and slid the cigarette into a battered tin box which then disappeared into his jacket pocket, "Let me do the talking. Just smile and nod. Got it?"

Crowe said nothing.

"Schtum," murmured Harris, "Not. A. Fucking. Word,"

Crowe spied a bin in the lobby and jammed the crumpled envelope in it.

They rode the elevator up to the top floor. Floor after floor of glass panelled offices lay dormant. Occasional blinks from the CPU's were the only signs of activity.

A Kind of Drowning

"So, Teflon D's staring at ten years: possession of an unlicensed firearm, possession of a class A narcotic, kidnap, conspiracy to commit murder, breaches of the jet-ski bye-laws 2006, and assault of a Garda Motorcycle Officer during the course of his arrest," said Harris, "Heard they tasered Teflon to fuck on the Belfast Road,"

"Those gimp twins fucked off to Spain to be with *'Their mammy'*, though," replied Crowe.

"We think the Spanish will play ball with us; fast-track the extradition request. Their solicitors are complaining about data protection bollocks, but we think your two recordings will be admissible. You'd want to see the shit DigitalFIRE pulled off the boyo's laptops scary fucking stuff,"

"Anything like their Spotify playlists?" said Crowe.

"Hilarious. Dark web, identity theft, bitcoin, crypto currency transactions. Their fingerprints were on the Nike, and Hunt's testimony they're facing manslaughter," said Harris.

"what about their daddy?" asked Crowe.

"Criminal Assets Bureau had a field day with poor old Teflon – yacht, houses up for sale the proceeds all siphoned into the National Emergency Fund. They even shot his dog when it attacked them. Vet pronounced it dead at the scene. Job done,"

Harris turned to stare at him just as the elevator stopped.

"You got your shit together, Podge. You got your hands dirty doing some honest graft getting this lot. You did some good."

Crowe felt some sense of justice had been served for Thea.

But it wasn't enough.

"Did Thea's mobile phone ever turn up?" he asked.

A Kind of Drowning

"No," murmured Harris.

Waiting for the elevator doors to open, Crowe slowly counted down from ten.

At the far end of the corridor in a large office were Townsend and O'Suilleabháin, sitting several feet apart, staring out at them stony faced through the glass,

"At least we don't have to shake their hands," said Crowe.

"Townsend would rip it off and feed the wet end to you," said Harris.

O'Suilleabháin as usual, sat rigid, not a button out of place. Stephanie Townsend, severe and crisp in her business attire was talking on her mobile. Her mouth moved slowly; her eyes stared at them. A line of disposable cups, a carafe of water and hand sanitisers stood in the middle of the table. Her laptop was closed. This time, there was no-one taking notes, no recorder or camera.

"Why are we here?" asked Harris. He gave the sanitisers two brisk pumps. He worked the gel in and around his fingers, "This could have been done over ZOOM?"

Crowe used the heel of his hand to squash out some gel. Townsend ended her call and aligned the phone with her laptop and brown folder with measured efficiency.

"No, it couldn't Mr. Harris - I'll be brief, Mr. Crowe," said Townsend, "Minister Gartland has reviewed your case, and your actions during your suspension – now…" she lasered her eyes down the folder's contents, "…I believe, at four months?"

Her eyes flicked up at Crowe and slid along to Harris. Probing for a response that would never happen, she continued,

A Kind of Drowning

"It's only thanks to O'Suilleabháin, Harris, and Dr. Olivia Cutts petitioning Minister Gartland and the Garda Commissioner that you are even sitting in this room. You are very lucky that the missing running shoe belonging to Thea Farrell was found. A one in a million chance, Crowe."

Crowe said nothing. He switched glances between them.

Harris spired his fingertips and stared at the neatly trimmed tips,

"Can you get to the point?" said Harris.

O'Suilleabháin cleared his throat.

"We have read your Occupation Health Report," he glanced down at the opened out folder, his pen tracing over to the salient points, "You have been officially cleared for duty, Garda Inspector Crowe."

Crowe noted the tone from his superior, like he could suddenly smell sour milk. The hurling scar curving up from his upper lip danced a tic.

"But it recommends on-going counselling sessions," continued O'Suilleabháin.

He barely contained his smirk.

"Hardly practical in this current climate," said Townsend. She made her signature derisory snort.

She continued "Mr. Moore, the football coach you hospitalised, has dropped all charges against you and An Garda Siochana. Seems he made a fraudulent claim for a car accident that was challenged and upheld in favour of the insurance company during his convalescence."

Her cold eyes looked up from the dossier and bored into Crowe.

"I hope we're not going to see any more of these incidents, Garda Inspector?"

Harris held a hand up before Crowe could find his voice,

"We would need a written guarantee that this is the end of the matter. That my colleague here is reinstated to his full rank and his salary back-dated," said Harris. His voice had lost its reedy twang and now rumbled across the table.

"And that all records of this investigation and disciplinary action both hard and soft-copy are quashed and purged. Otherwise we get up and walk away," he continued.

Who'd have thought Harris had grown a pair of balls, thought Crowe.

O'Suilleabháin's expression gave nothing away.

Which meant he had something. Some titbit of information; an ace in the hole.

"Without doubt, Inspector Crowe's actions were instrumental in bringing a serious criminal to justice. His actions too have brought Ephraim Hunt and his activities into the frame. CAB have indicated the proceeds from Cosgrave's operations alone yielded over €20 million, as well as cocaine, heroin, and cannabis resin with an estimated street value of €25 million. Considering what we found at his residences which included a collection of bespoke Gränsfors Bruk throwing axes in one of the basements, we took a particularly sinister yahoo off the street."

"Will he be prosecuted for the murder of Thea Farrell," said Crowe, "He called her 'collateral damage',"

"That's for the Director of Public Prosecutions to decide on," replied O'Suilleabháin, "Take some heart from what we uncovered thanks to you,"

"What about Hunt? The prints we pulled from the cigar tube?" said Crowe.

"He's co-operating with us, he admitted he was on the island though his testimony is weak due to his mental state at the time. He did confirm when cautioned the information about Cosgrave and his sons. Garda Technical found traces of his DNA near a mooring post, blood, that put Hunt on the island recently,"

"…and?" began Crowe,

"We're working on Desmond Cosgrave and awaiting an extradition deal from Spain,"

Fuck you, O'Suilleabháin, thought Crowe. His jaw clenched and unclenched,

"With respect, sir, that's a fucking betrayal to the Farrells," said Crowe, "Those clowns do time for unrelated crimes even though they murdered a nineteen year old woman,"

"Sometimes the bad guys win, Crowe. You know that" said O'Suilleabháin.

Crowe stared ahead now. He could feel his temples beginning to coil.

Townsend leaned forward, the harpy at his dinner,

"That's all well and good, but when stacked up against the damage to the reputation of the force, the Minister feels we behaved correctly in suspending Garda Crowe. We will not expunge the records or back date your pay. However, due to the national crisis we are facing; under 'The 2020 Health Preservation and Protection and Other Emergency Measures in the Public Interest Act', Inspector Crowe is required to return to duty. It's all hands on deck, gentlemen. The government has reactivated the '1947 Health Act' and we have an obligation to the safety of the public on this island. The suspension is lifted due to exceptional circumstances, but no, Mr Harris, his pay will not be back-dated, nor the record purged. He is in effect on a one-year written final warning."

She closed the folder with swift finality.

"One more infraction and you are out, Crowe. Now, any other questions?"

Crowe knew it. Harris knew it and O'Suilleabháin knew it too. THE BIG MACHINE had spoken, and a backlog of six months of cases beckoned.

"No. No other questions," said Crowe.

"Well, Garda Inspector Crowe," said O'Suilleabháin's, "let's get back to work, shall we? IT will reinstate your passwords and unlock your computer, you're back on duty day after tomorrow."

"Yes, Chief Superintendent," replied Crowe.

As he left the room, something occurred on him, something omitted.

"Cosgrave was carrying a concealed weapon. A Walther P99. Was it recovered?" he asked.

"No weapon was recovered during his arrest, Crowe. Now, I'm sure you'll all agree, I think we're done here?" said O'Suilleabháin.

"We are, Chief Superintendent," replied Crowe.

A Walther P99 was a standard-issue Garda sidearm.

***

Crowe purchased a coffee at the stall in Connolly Station. As he tore three sugar sachets with his teeth whilst juggling the lid and the piping hot beverage in both hands, he looked up at the pulsing information display. His train, the 14:20, was delayed. Advertising screens tried to bring a little colour to the cavernous gloom of the station; they flashed bright cheery commercials in booming loops. Pigeons scraped and hobbled around searching for scraps. On the far side of the tracks, two old ladies sat with disposable masks slung under their chins as they chatted. Their shopping bags were piled like a treasure trove. He pulled out his last cigarette and turned the coffee lid over as a makeshift ashtray. He smoked and sipped. The breeze cut like a knife and smelled of the Liffey.

Two DARTs passed either side of the platform before his inter-city train arrived. The ladies boarded the second one.

The inter-city was deserted. Crowe eased himself into a window seat and leafed through an abandoned tabloid starting from the back pages and skimming through to the front. The graffitied walls, sidings and dilapidated engine sheds slipped past as the train wound its way out of Dublin. It picked up pace and hurtled past the back gardens of terraced houses and clipped through the junctions until the sea appeared. Crowe folded his arms and closed his eyes and let the rhythm of the journey lull him. He savoured the momentary peace, his thoughts for once had stilled and he allowed himself the luxury of rest. He felt whole again.

It was only as the sweeping bay of Roscarrig appeared that Crowe opened his eyes. The station carpark was empty and as he stepped onto the platform he pulled out his mobile and dialled,

"Harris, are you busy?"

A Kind of Drowning

Echoes

There is no word in the English language for a parent that suffers the death of a child. Because the concept alone is beyond words. A hole had been punched in Grace Farrell's universe, a great gaping maw that absorbed and crushed all available light. The most basic things in her life became a daily struggle. Her concentration was fragmented, as if two TV shows were playing alongside each other simultaneously. Neighbour's faces became unfamiliar and their voices seemed strange as they spoke to her.

But the mind finds ways to compensate.

Grace found herself answering a question from Thea. She could hear Thea sometimes, humming a song in the other room in her mind. Sometimes the house would settle as the temperature changed and Grace thought she could hear her in her bedroom or see Thea standing in her peripheral vision. Constant and moving through every waking hour of the day.

Grace thought she heard Thea laugh, she looked around, but the kitchen was empty. The house was empty. The house was dead; nothing but furniture and accumulated clutter. Thea was dead, buried in the cold, hard soil of Roscarrig. It was the one thing above all that she missed: Thea's laughter.

In her nightmares, Grace could see Thea clawing for air, sinking into the heartless depths, and calling out 'Mam' over and over in a halo of air bubbles. But the coroner and the forensic expert had said that Thea was unconscious when she drowned. That there would have been no awareness – but then Grace would gladly plug her visions into their skulls to tell them they were talking shite. Because when Grace woke screaming, she could make out the silhouette of Thea at the foot of the bed whispering *'Mammy'*.

She remembered how Thea was terrified of water as a toddler.

A Kind of Drowning

"Did I push her too hard?" said Grace aloud.

It was as much a question as a cry of pain.

The tap dripped.

The odds had been stacked against her from the moment she had been born and Grace decided to tip the balance. From sitting on the steps of the pool in her tiny yellow water wings, Thea had begun to take her first swimming lessons. Expensive. Thea, under the tutelage of Fran, her instructor armed with a long, aluminium pole, learned to push off the bar with her feet. Thea learned to Fran's shouts of,

"1-2-3, left arm up. 1-2-3, wrist turn, 1-2-3, left arm into the water. Right arm repeat. Brilliant Thea!, let's go again, brilliant sweetheart,"

The aluminium pole would gently nudge Thea back into the centre of the lane. Soon it wasn't needed. From widths to lengths and Fran's cajoling and encouragement, Thea Farrell became a silver medal winner.

The sink had overflowed again, spilling suds onto Grace's jeans and flip-flops. It pooled around the kitchen units. She turned off the tap but if felt like someone else's hand moving in slow motion. Andrew had complained that the laundry was piling up, the house was dirty and coming home from a hard day was depressing.

Perhaps they should get a cleaner in? But Andrew had replied "You're home all day?"

Home all day. Every day for the nineteen years of Thea's life. Nineteen beautiful years full of hugs and laughter, kisses, and tears. Flying out from Dublin all around Europe, watching Thea compete for Ireland.

All gone. Gone for good.

A Kind of Drowning

Grace was prescribed drugs; she didn't take them. She needed to be focussed, sharp. Andrew wanted her to keep on top of the invoices and tax returns. He was out slaving away; it was the least she could do.

It was his way of processing grief, she considered. Two days after the funeral he was back to work, travelling from building site to the builder's providers.

Working through it. That's what you do, Grace, work through it. Leaving at 7:30am six days a week and returning twelve hours later, as regular as clockwork.

He hated the radio on. Preferred the silence. Attempts at conversation were met with sullen monotone. He told her not to call him during the day unless it was urgent.

As if a dead child wasn't reason enough.

Now that Dublin was in lockdown, his mood had blackened further. Grace had faced him down over breakfast. Their marriage had always been tempestuous, on occasion he had hit her, and she had hit back, never giving an inch. He blamed it on the pressure, the weight of ended expectations and she had acted in self-defence.

Grace sighed a long low breath.

She went to the utility room where the washing machine and tumble dryer were now inactive. She found the mop and the bucket and looked out at the garden. The lawn was unkempt, and the fences needed painting. It felt like she was living in a forever twilight. She felt utterly alone.

She stared at the large shed at the back of the garden, built by Andrew and his father, Andrew Snr., both lean and wiry men who handled tools with innate ease. The garden and the shed were Andrew's domain and Grace always felt like a guest when they would fire up the barbecue.

A Kind of Drowning

But the barbecue was now under wraps and the weeds were running amok.

Andrew Snr., hadn't dealt well with a Down Syndrome granddaughter. Perhaps he had had too much influence on his son,

"A waste of metal," he'd commented on Thea's silver medals. Andrew didn't speak up. Hadn't challenged. Hadn't protected. Hadn't travelled to the Olympics and missed out on a wonderful, awe-inspiring event. Thea had outshone both the Farrells and neither of them had liked it. At the old bastard's funeral, she had laughed and danced internally while pretending to help her husband with his grief.

Bloody good riddance.

The doorbell jarred her to life.

She looked at the clock; how long had she been standing here?

Grace opened the front door, one of the girls from two doors down, Lauren the waitress from the Boogie-Woogie stood with a Pyrex dish covered with a lid.

"Howya doin' Mrs F?" she asked.

Grace forced a smile, but it didn't reach her eyes,

"I'm ok. Thank you."

Lauren held out the dish,

"Mam made this for you. You can drop it back whenever. She has an ulterior motive though," Lauren grinned, "We were opening a bottle of Rosé and the cork fell apart, may we borrow a pliers please?"

Grace motioned her to come in.

A Kind of Drowning

"Just pop it on the table, Lauren," said Grace as she walked through the kitchen and out into the garden. It was only then that Grace noticed that the shed door was open.

She would get the blame.

Grace trudged along the path to the shed. She tugged on the overhead lights. Inside were long shelves full of power tools and stacked wood and scaffolding. At the far end was a workbench complete with a manual vice, and above, saws of various sizes hanging regimentally.

She scanned the hanging tools but there were no pliers. Andrew always kept two tool boxes: one in the van and one below the workbench. She found it. A big metallic one, she dragged it out and hoisted it onto the bench.

She prised the compartments open, screwdrivers were aligned neatly, boxes of screws, nails and rawl plugs glistened, ready to deploy. She was about to fish in the main compartment when she froze.

There was an iPhone in the toolbox.

Grace took it and held it up. The screen was cracked, and the casing was chipped. It had the briny tang of the sea about it. There were grains of sand in the grooves and nicks. It was only when she turned it over that she realised it was Thea's.

Garfield grinned back with a cartoon leer as he clawed the back of the phone.

Her thumb pressed the home key and the shattered phone flickered into life. The battery life fragmented in the corner displayed **100%**.

Which meant it had been recently recharged. Grace pulled open drawers, tore down tools and ducked below the workbench looking for an electrical socket.

It was only when Lauren appeared at Grace's side that she realised she was screaming.

Screaming at the top of her lungs…

THE END

©2021 Robert Craven

Author Bio

Robert Craven has been writing short stories and novels since 1992.

His Wartime of Eva series: Get Lenin, Zinnman**,** A Finger of Night**,** Hollow Point and Eagles Hunt Wolves have received rave reviews and garnered four and five-star reviews on both Amazon and Kobo platforms. Get Lenin is now an audiobook @Audible and all good audio platforms.

His Sebastian Holt novel 'The Road of a Thousand Tigers' released in 2018 went to No.#1 on Kobo downloads during the summer of 2019 in Canada, Australia and New Zealand.

A former touring musician, he also regularly reviews CDs for Independent Irish Review Ireland.

Robert is a member of the Irish Writer's Union, and lives in Dublin.

Website

https://www.robert-cravenauthor.ie/

Author's note

This book wouldn't have happened without the clear headed editing by my wife, Fiona. The process began in October 2019 through 2020, notching up 14 versions to this one. Her insights, push backs and at times, ruthless edits were invaluable, and I learned to both respect and fear her green biro. From the very outset she was supportive, encouraging, and impatient.

And she had to put up with me.

April 2021

A Kind of Drowning

A Kind of Drowning